WINTER IN IRELAND

PAMELA M. KELLEY

CHAPTER 1

Jennifer Graham studied her boyfriend's profile while his attention was glued to his iPhone. They were at Delancey's in downtown Beauville for dinner. Jen doubted if Paul was actually aware of the significance of the date. He'd simply texted her earlier in the week to confirm dinner, as usual, on Saturday night and told her to pick the place. Delancey's seemed appropriate as it was where they'd had their first date, exactly one year before.

She still found him every bit as attractive physically as she had when they first met. She supposed that he was her type, if she had one. Thick, blond hair, blue eyes, an easy smile. Tall, just over six feet, and lean. He didn't work out much. He was too busy for that and his nervous energy easily burned off whatever he ate—when he remembered to eat.

Paul was a junior attorney at the top law firm in Bozeman and to be fair, he had warned her when they first met that he was on the partner track and worked long hours. In his next breath, though, he'd promised that he wouldn't let work rule his life, that he understood the importance of having an off button. But apparently, that didn't apply to his phone, which was on 24/7 and seemed to rule his life.

"I thought you were going to put that away during dinner,"

Jen said softly as the waiter brought their meals out. Shrimp scampi for her and a New York Strip steak for him.

"I'm sorry." He hit send, put the phone face down on the table and flashed her the shy smile that usually won her over.

"How was your day?" he asked as he cut into his steak.

Jen picked up her fork and played with her pasta, twirling the buttery strands around, as she waited for it to cool. "I finished the book today. First draft, anyway. But the editing shouldn't take too long." She felt like celebrating. Finishing a book was a huge deal. She'd been immersed in her story world for the past few months and it was an emotional one. She was a romance writer and although it still needed some work, she had a tingly feeling that it was her best book yet. She hoped that her readers would agree.

"That's great." His phone vibrated again, and Jen watched him glance at it and then look away. She knew it was killing him not to at least check the caller ID.

"Super busy as usual?" she asked lightly.

He nodded. "One of the newer associates quit last week, so a lot of his work has been reassigned to me, until they hire someone new. I don't mind, though. The work is interesting." She knew he didn't mind. Paul lived and breathed his work. She'd half expected him to cancel their plans for tonight. He'd been doing that more often lately, always pleading a pressing work deadline.

"Are you going in tomorrow?"

"Yes. Sunday too, probably."

"Well, I'm glad you didn't cancel tonight."

He chuckled. "I almost did. But I figured you'd kill me after canceling last weekend."

"Yeah, I wouldn't have been happy about that. Especially today of all days."

A confused look came into his eyes and she knew that he had no idea what she was talking about.

She sighed. "It's our one-year anniversary today. That's why I suggested coming here."

He set his fork down and the apologetic smile was back. "I'm sorry. I should have realized that."

"It's all right." But it really wasn't. Not that he forgot the anniversary, Jen was less concerned about that than the fact that he just didn't have time for her. She wasn't any kind of priority in his world. And she had a feeling it would only get worse. Paul had told her that he was on the express track to partner which meant he could get there in five years instead of ten. He just wouldn't have much of a life during those five years. And neither would she.

Her scampi was delicious, though, and they ate in semi-comfortable silence. She knew that he was preoccupied with whatever it was that he was working on.

"So, I'm pretty sure that I'm going to go to Ireland. I'm thinking of staying for a month at least, maybe two."

"Ireland?" Paul yawned and took a sip of his beer.

"I told you this a few weeks ago, remember? That I was thinking of going there for a research trip? My next book is set in Dublin."

"Oh. Maybe you did mention that." His phone vibrated again. He touched it, but didn't flip it over.

"So, I'll be gone for two months, probably. Will you miss me?" He wasn't paying attention at all now and his phone was still buzzing.

"Just check it," she said shortly as the waitress came and cleared their plates. Jen ordered a coffee. Paul still had half a beer left. She got up to go to the ladies' room, and when she came back, Paul was still hunched over his phone, reading email.

"Do you want dessert?" she asked as she stirred a packet of sugar into her coffee.

"No, I'm good," he said, without even looking up.

Five minutes went by, while Jen sat there stewing. Finally, she did what she needed to do. She got her own phone out of her purse and sent a text message. She heard the ping when it was delivered and then a moment later, Paul put the phone down.

"You're mad."

"Not anymore. I meant what I said in the message. I'm done."

"Okay, I won't check my phone anymore. I'm sorry." He pulled a credit card out of his wallet and placed it on the bill.

"Doesn't matter anymore."

"Don't be like that. Let's go back to your place and celebrate our anniversary." Paul pulled out the easy smile again, the one that used to make her heart flutter. It didn't work anymore.

"I'm serious, Paul."

"You broke up with me through a text message?" Now he sounded pissed.

"It seemed the best way to get your attention. And it's not just a text message. I'm here in front of you, not that you've noticed." She took a sip of her coffee before adding, "This isn't working for me anymore, and I don't see it getting any better." She felt her eyes start to water and fought it back. "You know it's only going to get worse, Paul. I hardly ever see you as it is."

"But it won't be forever. Just a few years, then it will slow down. I'll be a partner."

"Will it? Maybe, maybe not. But it's too long for me."

They were both quiet for a moment. Finally, Paul spoke. "What if we got married? I was thinking we probably would in another year or so." He hadn't seen this coming and was now trying to negotiate.

Jen shook her head. "It's never been about getting married for me. It's about spending quality time with the right person."

"And you don't want that to be me?" He was sulking now. The evening had thrown him a curve ball, one he didn't have an easy answer for.

"I thought I did, actually. But that doesn't seem to be possible. I'm sorry, Paul."

He drove her home in silence and when they reached her condo, he tried once again. "Why don't I come in for a bit and we can talk this out, see if there's a way to make it work?"

Jen smiled sadly. "There's nothing left to say, Paul. I wish you all the best."

He pulled her in for a hug and kissed her forehead. Her tears came at his touch, flowing freely down her cheeks. She was glad for the darkness.

"I'm sorry," he said as she opened the car door. He waited until she was in her condo and then she watched him drive away. She grabbed a tissue and then found the emergency pint of Ben and Jerry's Cherry Garcia that she kept stashed deep in the freezer. She had wanted dessert, but this wasn't what she'd had in mind.

CHAPTER 2

Jennifer typed "The End" and reached for yet another tissue, dismayed to find the box was empty. It was a good sign that she was a sobbing mess, though. It meant her readers would probably like the book. She knew she was feeling a bit more emotional than usual, as her breakup with Paul was barely a week ago. She had really liked him. Paul was smart and though he wasn't the most handsome man in the room, he'd had a nice smile and warm eyes. But she hadn't realized right away how driven he was and how singular his focus. For too long, she had been feeling more lonely in that relationship than she had when she was single.

Although she still thought about him and missed him, not once had she regretted her decision to end things. She got up and went to the bathroom to grab a tissue and smiled at the sound of a knock on the door. Perfect timing. She dabbed her eyes quickly and then opened the door. Her next-door neighbor, Mandy Shores, stood there holding a chilled bottle of Prosecco.

"Are we ready to celebrate?" Mandy asked as she stepped inside the condo.

Jen laughed. "Yes. I just finished my final edits and am more than ready."

Jennifer took the bottle into the kitchen and opened it over the sink in case it was a little too bubbly. She poured them each a glass and they settled on the high stools that lined her kitchen island.

She'd bought her condo just a few years ago, on her twenty-ninth birthday. Her sister, Isabella, was a realtor and had handled the sale. Jen finally had it looking exactly the way she'd envisioned when she first bought it, but it had been a gradual process. She hadn't made all the changes at once. The kitchen had been first.

She loved to cook and the kitchen had been ugly and outdated, with orange Formica countertops that had prevented more than one sale. But, as her wise sister had told her, most of the fixing up the condo needed was easy cosmetic stuff—fresh paint, new fixtures, that kind of thing. But the kitchen was where she'd splurged.

Now the countertops were a gleaming quartz that looked like white marble, but was much stronger. Stainless steel appliances and creamy white cabinets gave it a modern look. She'd done the rest of the condo in soft shades of white and blue gray.

"How did the book turn out? Are you happy with it?" Mandy asked.

"I am. I think the readers will like it. I hope so, anyway."

Mandy took a sip of her wine and was quiet for a moment before asking, "Does it ever bother you? Writing something like that when things aren't going well in your own love life?"

"Sometimes," Jen admitted. "But I'm a hopeless romantic. I really believe that there's someone out there for everyone, and if you find that right person, you can have your happily ever after." She grinned and added, "Even though it seems like it's never going to happen for me."

"It will," Mandy assured her.

"Thanks. It will for you, too, I'm sure of it." Mandy had become one of Jen's closest friends over the past few years. They were about the same age and when Mandy had welcomed her when she moved in, they had felt like old friends immediately.

Mandy was striking with long, loose curls that were the most gorgeous golden caramel shade. She was an event planner at a hotel in Bozeman and had recently been promoted to a manager.

Her personal life wasn't going quite as well, however. She was also dealing with a recent break-up, though her situation was slightly different. A few months ago, she ended a three-year relationship with a charming golf instructor who wasn't ready to settle down. Yet, rumor had it that he was already engaged to someone else.

"Have you booked a place to stay yet?" Mandy asked.

"No, not yet. I'm having a hard time deciding between a hotel or small cottage."

Mandy's eyes lit up. "Good. I just hung up with my Aunt Sorcha before coming over here and mentioned that you're going to be spending a few months in Dublin. She insisted that you stay with her."

Jen had met Mandy's aunt a few years back and really liked her, but it seemed like too big of an imposition.

"I don't know. Would she really want me underfoot that long?"

"Absolutely. She sounded excited about it actually. She lives alone now, in a good-sized house just outside of Dublin. It's a great location, and I think she's a bit lonely. She's good company."

"She seems like she would be." The idea was growing on Jen, and it would save her a good bit of money, too. "Are you really sure she wouldn't mind? I'd be happy to pay her whatever the going rate might be."

Mandy laughed at the idea. "She won't take your money and would be insulted at the mere mention of it. I'll tell her you're confirmed."

"All right, if you're sure?"

"Consider it done. I am going to miss you, though."

Jen sighed. "I know. I'll miss you, too. I won't know a soul there, except for your aunt, and I doubt she's going to want to join me at the local pub."

Mandy chuckled. "Not very likely. She doesn't drink much. A cup of tea in the garden is more her style."

"Well, that sounds lovely, too."

Mandy took a slow sip of wine and said, "I bumped into Paul last night, at the market. I ran in quick to grab some milk and eggs." She was quiet for a moment. "He asked about you. He looked terrible. Tired and sad, confused even. Almost as if he doesn't know what happened."

Jen sipped her wine and thought about Paul. She did feel badly that he was having a hard time with the break-up. "He knows, but I don't think he really understands. We had fun when we saw each other, but it was so infrequent. On our last date, he spent the whole night checking email on his phone. And he saw nothing wrong with it."

Mandy shook her head.

"Lots of people do that. I think it's just awful."

Just knowing that Mandy ran into Paul helped to confirm Jennifer's decision to go abroad for a while. It would be easier to move on and get over him if she didn't have to worry about bumping into him.

"Does your aunt have any children?" Jennifer thought she remembered mention of a son or two, but she had come alone when she'd visited.

"Two sons, Tim and Ian, both in their mid-thirties. Tim just moved out a year ago and Ian has been gone for years. He has a condo in the city. He runs some sort of tech company and sounds like he's even more of a workaholic than Paul."

Jen chuckled. "So he probably won't want to go to the pubs, either."

"No, but Tim might. He has a job with normal hours and lives just a few miles away. I bet he'd love to show you around."

Mandy left a few hours later, after they'd polished off a plate of homemade nachos and most of the Prosecco. Jen cleaned up the dishes and then curled up on her favorite comfy sofa in the living room to read for a bit. She pulled a soft blanket around her and gazed around the room. She was excited to travel, to get away for a while, but Jen was a home-body at heart. She loved being home, near family and friends.

Jen sighed. She finally had her condo looking exactly the way she wanted and now she was heading to Ireland for several months. But at least she knew she'd eventually have her oasis of calm to come home to.

CHAPTER 3

Jen looked around the table in her mother's kitchen. Everyone was there, her mother, her husband Tom, who she'd been married to for just over ten years now, her sister, Isabella, and Uncle Jim. He was really their great uncle and was one of her favorite people in the world. She would probably miss him the most. Uncle Jim was in his early nineties but had more energy than most people she knew.

It was hard to believe that she was heading off to Ireland in the morning. The last few weeks had flown by. Her mother had insisted that everyone come for dinner to give her a proper sendoff.

"Maybe I'll hop on a plane and come visit you. It's been a long time since I've been anywhere. Why not start with Ireland?" Uncle Jim teased.

"I'd love that!" Jen doubted he'd actually make the trip, but his health was good, so there was no reason why he couldn't travel if he wanted to.

"Did you leave contact information for me? A home phone number for where you'll be staying?" her mother asked as she set a bowl of mashed potatoes in the middle of the table, followed by a platter of sliced roast beef.

"I did. It's a folded sheet of paper by the phone. I'll have my cell with me, too, so you can always reach me that way."

After they finished dinner and the dishes were cleared, Isabella surprised her by disappearing for a moment and then reappearing carrying a gorgeously frosted chocolate cake topped with lots of pink candles, all glowing merrily. Her mother followed close behind with a stack of dessert plates and forks. She set the cake in front of Jen as everyone sang *Happy Birthday*, and then her mother handed her a big knife. As Jen cut the slices, Isabella spoke. "I know it's tomorrow, but since you won't be here, we figured we'd celebrate early and send you off on your trip at the same time. We all chipped in to get you this." Isabella reached behind her chair and then handed Jen a pretty carry-on bag.

"Oh, thank you! I was thinking about buying a piece just like this."

"Look inside, there's more," her mother said.

Jen unzipped the bag and reached in. She drew out several pair of stretchy travel pants and soft tops that would be great for layering, along with a few pretty sweaters and a new pair of pajamas. She felt her eyes grow misty. It was very sweet of them and totally unexpected. She got up and hugged both her sister and mother and thanked them.

"It was our pleasure, dear," her mother said happily.

"It really was fun to shop for you. I may have picked up a few of these things for myself, too," Isabella admitted.

"So what else is new?" Uncle Jim teased. He knew that was how both of them often shopped, as they had similar taste.

"I picked you up a little something, too." He handed her a flat, wrapped package.

She opened it, and immediately leaned over and gave him a hug and kiss on the cheek.

"I absolutely love it! Thank you so much." He'd given her a soft, leather-bound journal and what looked like an expensive, fancy pen to write in it.

"If you do your first draft in that, you'll never have to worry about losing data," he said with a grin.

Jen smiled. "That's true. This is really wonderful. I'll bring it on the plane with me and jot down ideas for my next book, and maybe use it as a journal, too, of my time in Ireland."

She glanced around the room. "Thank you so much, everyone. I almost don't want to leave now."

"I wish I'd had the chance to do this. It's an incredible opportunity." Jen's mother smiled as she collected the empty plates from the table. "You'll be back before you know it, dear."

"Just make sure you come home. Don't you go off and marry an Irishman," Uncle Jim said sternly, but there was a twinkle in his eye.

She laughed. "That is one thing I can say with absolute certainty that you will not have to worry about. This is purely a research trip. Another relationship is the last thing I am looking for right now."

CHAPTER 4

Jen spotted Mandy's Aunt Sorcha once she got off the plane, through customs and luggage and into the arrivals area. Her strawberry-blonde hair was a little shorter than she remembered, but she recognized the bouncy curls, wire-rimmed glasses and big smile. Aunt Sorcha was a short, round woman, wearing a pretty yellow top and gray dress pants. She pulled Jen in for a hug as soon as she reached her.

"How are you, dear? Are you hungry? Let's go get your bags. I've got the car parked in the garage." The questions came fast and furious and after Jen assured her that she was good and not starving, Aunt Sorcha led the way to collect her luggage and after stowing both bags in the car, they were off. She kept up a steady stream of chatter and insisted that Jen call her Aunt Sorcha as well.

"It will just be easier, don't you think?" Without waiting for an answer, she continued talking.

"Everyone wants to meet you. Gracie may pop over for tea. She's my best friend in the world and lives around the corner. She'll probably have a fresh batch of ginger scones to welcome you. You'll meet the others soon enough." Jen nodded, smiled and tried to keep up. Aunt Sorcha seemed to have a lively social life. As she pulled into the driveway, she added, "My son Tim said he'd try to come around later and if you're not too tired, he'll take you to the pub down the road for a welcome drink."

"That would be wonderful." Jen knew it would take her a few days to get used to the time difference. Dublin was eight hours ahead of Montana and it still felt early in the day to her.

"Oh, and I'm not sure when you'll meet him as he's always working, but Ian, my oldest, is going to be staying with us for a few weeks. The pipes burst in his building and made a mess, so he's having it fixed and remodeled at the same time. He's going to stay in the little apartment over the garage."

"He can have my room if he'd rather. I could take the apartment if that would be easier for you both?" Jen felt guilty that she might be displacing her son.

"That's sweet of you, but Ian actually prefers the apartment. It's where he lived before he bought his condo. There's no kitchen, though, so you might see him now and again in the main house, especially on the weekends that he has Ella. She's six and the cutest little thing you ever did see."

Jen grabbed both of her bags and followed Aunt Sorcha into the house.

"Your room is at the end of the hall. Why don't you get settled and I'll make us a cup of tea?"

"Perfect, thank you." Jen brought her bags into her assigned room and looked around. It was a large, spacious room and had a cozy feel to it. There was a pale yellow quilt on the queen-sized bed that was topped with several pillows. A rocking chair sat in a corner, next to a window that looked out over a grassy back yard with a small garden. She set her bags on the bed and unpacked a little, hanging up a few items on the empty hangers in the closet and stashing some of her sweaters in an empty drawer. She could take her time with the rest later.

When she returned to the kitchen, Aunt Sorcha was just pouring hot tea into two cups. Jen turned at the sound of a knock at the front door.

"Oh, that must be Gracie. Could you let her in?"

Jen opened the door and was immediately swept into a hug by a large woman balancing a tray of scones.

"You must be Jennifer! I'm Gracie. She told you about me?"

"She did. It's nice to meet you."

Gracie breezed in, and Jen shut the door behind her and followed her into the kitchen.

"You must be starving after traveling all day. Have a scone. It will take the edge off. They're still warm."

Gracie bustled around the kitchen, gathering a few small plates from a cupboard and setting them on an island next to the scones. She took one, put it on a plate and slid it toward Jen.

"Thank you. They look delicious." Jen took a bite and savored the gingery sweetness of the scone.

Aunt Sorcha poured tea for Gracie and they sat around the kitchen for the next hour, chatting about everything under the sun. Gracie stood to go just as the front door opened.

"I need to get home to get supper on the table for Michael. It was a pleasure to meet you, Jen."

"Oh, Tim's here," Aunt Sorcha exclaimed as a tall, thin man with a warm smile walked into the room and gave her a hug.

"Tim, this is Jennifer, Mandy's friend from Montana."

"Great to meet you, Tim."

"How's Susie doing?" Aunt Sorcha asked as Tim reached for a scone.

"She's good." He looked at Jen. "She would have come, too, but tonight is her ceramics class. I'm on my own for a few hours."

"Why don't you take Jen to the pub for a beer?" Aunt Sorcha suggested.

"I'd love to. There's one right up the road, if that sounds good to you?" he asked.

"Oh, that sounds wonderful. Would you like to join us?" Jen asked Aunt Sorcha, who laughed.

"My pub days are long over. You kids go and have fun, though."

CHAPTER 5

I an Shepard rubbed his eyes and checked the time on his computer. It was half past five, a normal quitting time for most, but far earlier than he usually ended his day. This past week especially had been a succession of late nights as his team worked overtime to ensure a successful release for their newest software product. They'd anticipated every potential problem, found and fixed the bugs early on, and this release was the smoothest in his young company's history. He could actually leave at a decent hour and surprise his mother by coming home before she retired to bed. Going to bed early sounded like a great idea to him.

He was just shutting down his computer when Callum, his CTO and best friend, poked his head in the office, wearing a grin.

"Don't forget, you're coming with us for a celebratory drink." Cal had been a university classmate and Ian credited much of the company's success to Cal's gift with all things technical. Ian was a strong programmer, too, but his ability was more with designing new products and managing the business side of things, while Cal made sure the underlying technology was sound, that the products worked with everything else. Ian had completely forgotten that he'd agreed to go for drinks once the product had successfully shipped. The last thing he felt like doing was going out to a bar and socializing. His energy was drained and a soft bed was far more appealing. But this was a milestone, and he knew it was important for the team.

"Of course I didn't forget! It's been too long. Where are we off to, then?"

"We thought maybe MacGregor's, if that works for you? It's close to your mother's place and more than half the team lives out that way. Better to be closer to home if we decide to have an extra pint.

"Perfect."

Cal left and Ian shut down his computer. MacGregor's wouldn't be so bad. At least it was on his way home. He could make an appearance, have a pint and be on his way.

CHAPTER 6

J en liked Tim instantly. He was friendly and easy to talk to. When they walked into his favorite local pub, several people called out 'hello' and the bartender gave him a wave as he approached the bar.

"I know what you'll be having. What about your lady friend?" He held out his hand towards Jen as he said, "Simon MacGregor. Welcome to my bar."

"Simon, this is Jen. She's visiting us from the States."

Simon smiled as he poured a pint of frothy draft beer and slid it towards Tim. "We have just about every kind of beer you can think of. What's your pleasure?"

Jen looked around the bar. None of the beers looked familiar. It didn't really matter to her. "I'll have what Tim's having."

"An excellent choice."

Jen wasn't much of a beer drinker. She usually preferred wine, but she tentatively took a sip of her freshly poured beer and it was good. Especially after the very long day of traveling.

Tim found seats for them at the far end of the bar and they settled in to enjoy their drinks. The crowd seemed to be a mix of ages, lots of people who looked like they had just gotten off work and stopped in on their way home.

"If you get hungry, the fish and chips and steak and ale pie here are great," Tim said as the smell of fried food wafted over. They chatted for the next twenty minutes or so, and he told her all about the neighborhood and suggested different places for her to be sure to visit. He also made her laugh as he told her about his wife's crazy pregnancy cravings. They were expecting their first child in a few months.

"She never was this addicted to ice cream before," he said as his phone rang. He glanced down at the caller ID and smiled.

"Speak of the devil. If you'd excuse me for just a minute, I'm going to go outside to take this." He slid off his chair and disappeared out the front door. Jen leaned back against the bar and watched the crowd as she sipped her beer. A few minutes later, a small group of men walked in and surveyed the room. When several of the people next to her got up at once to leave, the men made their way over quickly to claim their seats. They all looked to be in an especially good mood, almost as if they were celebrating something.

As a writer, Jen liked to study people and try to figure them out. She wasn't always right, but she was often close. The way people dressed, their mannerisms, body language—it all fascinated her. She took another sip of her beer and was surprised to see it was almost three quarters gone. Simon had noticed, though. He appeared at her side as she set down her glass.

"Almost ready for another?"

Jen glanced toward the door for a moment. Tim had been gone for at least five minutes and who knew how much longer he'd be.

"Sure, why not?"

"Have you been abandoned, then?" The voice next to her sounded amused. Jen looked up and caught her breath as a pair of intense blue eyes locked on to hers. His smile sent laugh lines dancing around his mouth and eyes. Thick dark hair and a hint of shadow along his jaw gave him a slightly scruffy but still clean-cut look that was very appealing. For a moment, Jen forgot that she'd decided she was off men, and enjoyed the view.

She smiled. "It seems that way, doesn't it? Must be a very important phone call."

He leaned against the bar and took a sip of his beer before saying, "Seems foolish to me. He could be here with you."

Jen chuckled. "It's not like that. He's just a friend."

His only reply was a look of doubt. One of his friends tapped his shoulder and he turned for a moment. She couldn't hear what they were saying, but the one talking paused to give high fives all around. Jen sipped her beer as she watched them. There were six of them, and they seemed a happy bunch.

"Are you celebrating something?" she asked when he turned back her way. She was curious to see if she was right.

He looked surprised. "We are, actually. A new release just shipped today and so far, no problems."

"Congratulations! That must be a good feeling." Jen took a sip of her beer.

"It is. I'm Ian, by the way."

"Jennifer, but I go by Jen."

He held out his hand. "It's nice to meet you."

Her hand felt small in his. His grip was strong and she felt a curious buzz when their skin touched. She smiled to herself. The universe must be playing some kind of joke on her to have her feeling such strong physical chemistry now, of all times, though she had to admit, the attention felt nice. He looked at her curiously.

"Are you on holiday? I thought I picked up an accent —American?"

"Yes, I'm American. It's sort of a working vacation. I'm here for a few months."

His eyes lit up. "A few months? Well, you'll need someone to show you around, then. Unless your 'friend' is doing that?"

Before Jen could answer, Tim was back, full of apologies. "I'm so sorry. I know that was rude of me. I tried to make the call as short as I could."

"Tim? What are you doing here?" Ian looked confused as Tim settled back into his seat and picked up his beer.

Tim looked Ian's way in surprise. "Me? That's a better

question for you, I think. I don't remember the last time I saw you here."

"Where's Susie?" Ian asked as it started to make sense to Jen.

"She's home now. Got out of her class early and is not at all happy with me at the moment. She's out of mint chocolate chip ice cream and apparently needs some as soon as possible." He looked Jen's way apologetically. "She's a great girl, but the hormones sometimes make her a little crazy."

Ian looked as confused as Jen felt a moment ago.

"This must be your brother?" she asked Tim.

"Yes, of course. So rude of me. Ian, this is Jennifer. She's Mandy's writer friend who is staying with Mam for a few months. Mam did mention that to you?"

Ian took a long sip of his beer. Jen couldn't read his mood. She thought she saw flashes of irritation and amusement flash across his face.

"I'm sure she did. I've just been so focused on the release that it didn't register." He turned his attention to Jen. "Did my mother tell you I'm going to be staying there for a while, too?"

Jen felt suddenly nervous for some reason. "She said her son Ian would be staying with her, yes. I didn't make the connection until you and Tim started talking."

Tim looked at his watch and finished his beer in one big sip. He glanced at Jen's glass mug which was still more than half-full.

"Are you in a hurry?" Ian asked him.

"No, of course not," he said as Simon pointed toward his empty mug to ask if he wanted another. Tim hesitated and Jen knew he was anxious to go.

"I don't need to finish mine. We can head out if you like."

Tim's relief was evident. "You don't mind? That would be great."

Ian chuckled. "Go home to your wife. I'll drive Jen back. We're going to the same place, remember?"

"Oh, right. If you don't mind, that would be great." Tim

turned to Jen. "Is that all right with you? No need for you to rush on my account."

Jen hesitated for a moment and Ian jumped in. "Go. Jen just got here. I'm sure she's not in a rush to leave. I'll get her home safely."

Tim left, and Ian slid into his seat and one of his friends jumped into his. The bar was packed, so only half of them managed to secure bar stools. Ian introduced Jen to the five guys who worked with him, and they chatted for a few minutes. Then the guys started debating the merits of a new program they were developing and Ian turned his back to them and his attention to her.

"So, we're going to be roommates for the next few weeks, maybe longer, depending on how long this renovation takes." He looked amused at the idea.

"Your mother told me about the damage to your condo. That must be annoying to deal with."

He shrugged. "It's not so bad. There were a few changes I wanted to make anyway. This was just the push I needed to get it done. I'd put it off because I didn't want to leave the condo after just moving in. It's going to be worth it when it's done."

"What's it like?"

"I don't know if you'd like it. It's sleek, black and gray. Black stone in the kitchen, and stainless steel. Dark hard wood floors, lots of windows."

"It sounds lovely." It did sound beautiful, if a bit cold and clinical. "Maybe it needs a woman's touch?" she suggested.

"I'm not looking for that!" he snapped. "I'm too busy for a relationship." He was so suddenly defensive that Jen was taken aback and then annoyed.

"I wasn't suggesting myself for the job. I meant maybe your mother could give her two cents."

He relaxed and had the grace to look a little embarrassed.

"Sorry, I didn't mean to be short. It's just that people are always suggesting that I need a wife or a serious girlfriend. I did that once. It didn't work out and truthfully, I don't have the time or the interest to go there again."

"Really? So you don't date at all?" He was making himself sound like a hermit.

Ian chuckled. "Oh, I date. But I make it clear that it's just casual so no one gets any ideas. Or gets hurt."

Jen frowned. "And the women you date are okay with that? Really?" It sounded awful to her.

His grin faded. "I take it you wouldn't be?"

"No. That would be the last thing I'd want. I'm not casual about relationships. I just ended one, though, so I'm not in the market for anything anyway, even if I were open to that kind of thing. Which I'm not," she added for emphasis. The very thought of it made her feel sad.

"Bitter break-up? That's another reason I keep things casual. It avoids that kind of messiness." He took a sip of his beer and Jen shook her head. Was he really that cold and able to detach his feelings?

"Life is messy. Emotions, too, if you care about the people you're with. I cared about Paul. We were actually quite serious. But ultimately, it didn't work out." Jen paused and took a sip of her drink. "He was an attorney. On the partner track and married to his job. I was his mistress. He didn't have time for me. In five—or realistically, ten years—he might. I guess our timing was just off."

Ian didn't say anything to that. Instead, he waved Simon over and ordered another round for them.

Jen reached for the new beer, lifted her mug and smiled. "But at least I know now what I don't want."

"What's that?" Ian smiled and Jen tried not to focus on the laugh lines that she found so attractive.

"I will never date another workaholic again!"

Ian tapped his glass against hers and said, "Well, I guess that rules me out, then. Too bad. We could have had a fun few months." His eyes held a mischievous gleam.

Jen laughed. "Yes, you're definitely out. You'd be too busy to have fun anyway."

Ian put his beer down. "Well, since we're just going to be

friends, then, let's get to know each other better. I'm sure my mother told you about Ella?"

"Your daughter? Yes she did. She's six I think?

He fished into his wallet and pulled out a slightly dog-eared photograph of an adorable little girl with big eyes and light brown curls.

"She's amazing. You'll meet her soon. I have her every other weekend and a month in the summer."

His face lit up as he talked about his daughter, which made Jen question his earlier statements about not wanting a relationship. He clearly had wanted that, at one time.

"Were you married long?" she asked, sensing it might be a sensitive subject.

"Depends on how you define long. A month can be too long if you're with the wrong person." He looked lost in thought for a moment and then continued. "We dated for a long time, five years or so. Getting married was the logical next step. I loved her, or at least I thought I did at some point. But I worked even longer hours then and money was always tight. She worked, too, and spent more time with her co-workers than with me. We were on the brink of divorce when she got pregnant. But after a year, nothing had changed and after a four year separation, we went through with the divorce."

"So, it's an amicable split, then? That's good."

Ian ran his hand through his hair and took a moment before answering.

"I don't know if that's the right word. She remarried immediately. That four year separation is required here by law. My business took off soon after and I think she resents that."

"I'm sorry it didn't work out." Jen wasn't sure what else to say.

He smiled. "Well, as my mother would say, 'everything happens for a reason.' I'm probably not the easiest person to live with, either. So now you can understand why I prefer to keep things casual? I also don't want to bring Ella into it and have her get attached to someone and then things don't work out."

"That's understandable. I look forward to meeting her. I'm sure your mother is thrilled to have you and her home for a while."

"No doubt. She's a good girl, you'll see." He set his empty beer mug down as Jen stifled a yawn. The long day of traveling was catching up to her.

"Are you about ready to go?" he asked.

"Yes, I'm ready."

IAN LED HER OUT TO HIS CAR, A SLEEK BLACK BMW SEDAN. Jen slid into the passenger side and pulled the seatbelt tight. The seats were soft leather and she loved the luxurious feel of them.

"My mother teases me about this car. I'd always wanted a sportier car, though, and when we went public two years ago, it was the one thing I splurged on." He started the engine and they were home in ten minutes.

When they walked inside, there was a note on the kitchen table, letting them know there was a steak pie in the refrigerator they could heat up if they were hungry. Jen's stomach growled as she read the words. She hadn't been hungry at all earlier. Now she was suddenly starving.

"We never did eat, did we?" Ian asked as he got the pie from the refrigerator and set it on the counter. "Do you want some?" He already had pulled two plates out and was scooping pie onto one of them.

"Yes, I'd love some. Thanks." A few minutes later, after a quick zap in the microwave, they sat down at the kitchen table and ate in comfortable silence. The pie was delicious—tender, bite-sized pieces of steak in a rich, mushroom gravy, with carrots and potatoes in a stiff pastry crust. She inhaled it and set her fork down, feeling full and happy. Ian finished just a minute before she did and jumped up for a second helping.

"More for you, too?" he asked.

"No, I'm stuffed. I'm off to bed, I think."

"Good night, then." He grinned. "And if you change your mind, we could have a lot of fun while you're here."

Jen chuckled. "Good night, Ian."

CHAPTER 7

The house was quiet when Jen woke the next day. She was surprised when she checked her cell phone and saw that it was after eleven. She was usually an early riser, and was a little embarrassed to have slept so late. She scrambled out of bed, and made her way into the kitchen, craving coffee something fierce.

"Good morning, dear. Can I make you a cup of tea?" Aunt Sorcha was sipping tea and reading the paper at the kitchen table.

"Good morning. I'm sorry I slept so late. I don't, usually."

"I expected you would, given the time difference. It took me a few days to adjust last time I flew back from the States." She got up and went to the cupboard, then turned back to Jen.

"Or would you rather have coffee, dear? Ian got me one of those fancy Keurig machines for Christmas. It makes anything you want."

"Coffee would be wonderful, thank you."

"Sit down and relax. It'll be ready in a jiffy. There are left-over scones if you want something to nibble on or if you're hungry I could make some eggs?"

"A scone would be perfect. I don't usually eat much for breakfast."

"Help yourself, then. They're on the counter. Plates are in the cupboard."

Once Jen was settled at the table with her coffee and scone, Aunt Sorcha joined her.

"So, I know you're here to work, but I thought you might want to do a little sight-seeing first to get the feel of the place for your book."

"I'd love that." Jen had been hoping to see as much as possible while she was in Ireland and wasn't quite ready to dive into the writing yet.

"What's your story about? Do you know yet? Or do you figure it out as you go?"

Jen smiled. People were often fascinated about how she created her stories and where her ideas came from.

"I make most of it up as I go. All I know so far is the heroine is an American girl working overseas in the Dublin office for a software company that is headquartered in the US. She falls in love with her boss, the one in Ireland," she explained.

"Oh, that sounds wonderful. I love a good romance. So, after you eat and get dressed, we can head out."

"Perfect." Jen was fully awake now that the coffee had kicked in, and was looking forward to the day.

AUNT SORCHA WAS AN EXCELLENT TOUR GUIDE. SHE SHOWED Jen all around Dublin, pointing out important landmarks as they drove and visiting one of her favorite museums. They stopped for a late lunch at Brennan's, one of the local pubs that she said was the best around. When they finished eating, they both had hot tea and shared a slice of pie.

Aunt Sorcha kept up a running commentary all day, telling her about all the various people she might meet, their neighbors and friends. Jen had a pretty good memory but gave up trying to remember it all. It had been a lovely, relaxing day and they were just about to pay the bill and leave when suddenly

Aunt Sorcha seemed a bit flustered and sat up tall in her seat as a man about her age walked over to them.

"Sorcha, I thought that was you. Fancy running into you today."

"Hello, Frank. This is Jen, our houseguest from the States. Jen, Frank is one of our neighbors. He lives just around the corner."

"It's nice to meet you," Jen said politely and watched with interest at the shift in Aunt Sorcha's demeanor.

"I was just giving Jen a tour, showing her the sights," she told him.

Frank smiled. "Well, then it makes sense that you brought her here. This is the best pub in town."

Aunt Sorcha beamed. "I told her that. What brings you by?"

"I'm meeting Henry for a pint. He's a bit at loose ends since Sheila passed."

"Henry's another neighbor," Aunt Sorcha explained. "He lost his wife a few months ago."

Frank waved at someone sitting at the bar. "It looks like Henry beat me here. Stop by and say hello on your way out?"

"We will."

When Frank was out of earshot, Aunt Sorcha leaned in and spoke softly. "I'll introduce you to Henry when we leave. The poor guy is just lost. Terribly nice of Frank to take him under his wing." Aunt Sorcha looked thoughtful, then added, "Frank lost his wife Vera a little over a year ago. It was hard on him, too."

"How long has it been for you?" Jen asked.

Aunt Sorcha smiled sadly. "Five years now, if you can believe it. Hardest thing I've ever had to go through. Wouldn't have made it if not for the boys and great friends."

"What was he like, your husband?"

Aunt Sorcha lifted her cup of tea and took a sip as she gathered her thoughts.

"Gerry was everyone's friend. They all loved him, but no one more than me. We met at a dance, and on our second date, we went for ice cream and he told me he wanted to marry me." She smiled at the memory. "We both just knew. He asked me properly a few months later. Got permission from my father first, of course. We had a long, happy life together, and I still miss him."

"He sounds like a wonderful man." Jen was quiet for a moment and then asked, "Have you dated at all since then? Or thought about it?"

Aunt Sorcha dropped her spoon and it clattered on the table. "Dated anyone? I'm all done with all that, dear."

Jen paused and tried to guess Aunt Sorcha's age. She was still an attractive woman. She dressed nicely and had a spring in her step.

"You're what, in your early sixties?"

Aunt Sorcha nodded.

"That's still young. You have many years left. It might be fun to share them with someone." Jen smiled and asked, "What about Frank?"

Aunt Sorcha looked taken aback at the thought. "Frank? What about him?"

"He might be a nice person to date."

Aunt Sorcha chuckled and then dismissed the idea entirely. "I couldn't possibly date Frank. It's far too soon for him, for one thing, and for another—well, he's Frank. I've known him and his wife for many years. We were all close friends."

"Friendship is a good basis for romance."

"I don't know about that. Now, are you ready to go?" Aunt Sorcha pulled out some bills and laid them on the check, waving off Jen's offer to share the bill.

On the way out, she introduced Jen to Henry, who was pleasant enough, but Jen couldn't help noticing that Frank's attention was fully on Aunt Sorcha. If she didn't know better, she would have sworn the two of them were smitten with each other.

WHEN THEY REACHED THE HOUSE, IT WAS ABOUT A QUARTER past three.

"I'm making a big pot of meatballs for dinner tonight, so am going to start the sauce now so it has plenty of time to simmer."

"Can I help you?" Jen offered.

"No, thank you, dear. Rest up and relax. Oh, and both boys will be here tonight for supper. You'll meet Susie, too, Tim's wife. Ian will probably disappear soon after, though. He usually eats then goes up to his room to get back to work."

Of course he did. That's what Paul usually did, too. Pity, too, because Ian was charming otherwise. But, Jen reminded herself once again that it was probably for the best. The last thing she needed was to fall for someone in another country.

CHAPTER 8

A light knock on his slightly ajar office door drew Ian's attention away from the email he was reading. Merry, his executive assistant, stood in the doorway.

"Sorry to interrupt, but you asked me to remind you that you need to leave early today."

Ian scowled. He'd almost forgotten about dinner with the family.

"Thank you, Merry. You saved me." She was a godsend, and had been his right hand since he founded the company. He told her all the time that he'd be lost without her.

Merry closed the door and Ian hurriedly shut down his computer. Traffic was heavy and he was running about ten minutes late by the time he reached his mother's house. He wasn't surprised to see his brother's car in the driveway. Tim was always punctual. Ian usually was, too, unless he lost track of time while working. He shut off the engine and headed into the house, and had to admit he was curious to see their houseguest again.

He'd been both surprised and intrigued when the American girl he'd been chatting with at the pub turned out to be his mother's houseguest. He'd been instantly attracted. Jen was a pretty girl, with her long dark hair, petite build and friendly smile. He'd enjoyed talking to her. It was a pity that she wasn't inclined to partake in some fun while she was visiting.

That would have suited him perfectly, though he could understand how it wasn't wise while he was living under his mother's roof. But he would be back in his own place in a few weeks. Still, he had to respect that she didn't go for casual flings. Unfortunately, that's all he had to offer anyone. Maybe someday that would change, but for now, Ella and his work were his top priorities.

"Ian's here!" his mother called out as he walked in the front door. Everyone was in the kitchen, gathered around the table. Ian hugged both his mother and Susie hello, then helped himself to a root beer from the refrigerator and settled at the table across from Jen.

"How are you settling in? Do anything fun today?" he asked her. She looked just as cute as he remembered, in a soft pink sweater that made her cheeks look rosy.

Jen smiled. "We had a lovely day. Your mother let me sleep in to a shockingly late time, and then we went sight-seeing. She showed me all around Dublin and we had a late lunch at her favorite place."

"Brennan's?" he asked.

"That's the one," his mother confirmed. "Ian, bring this over to the table, would you?" He jumped up and took the bowl of pasta that his mother handed him. She followed him to the table with a steaming casserole dish full of red sauce and meatballs, then returned a moment later with a loaf of crusty garlic bread that had already been sliced.

His stomach grumbled and he realized he'd skipped lunch. He'd been so involved in his latest project that he hadn't even thought of eating. Merry often picked up a sandwich for him, but she knew not to bother him when he had his door shut, and he'd had it shut most of the day so he could focus. His mother settled into the empty chair next to him and everyone helped themselves to the food.

"How was your day?" Jen asked him as she tore off a piece of garlic bread and then popped it in her mouth. A bit of butter drizzled off her lip and he watched transfixed as she dabbed at it. Her eyes were half closed as she enjoyed the buttery bread.

"Ian? Jen asked you how your day was," his mother said as she reached for the shaker of parmesan cheese and sprinkled it over her meatballs.

"Sorry. It was good. Busy, as usual. We're working on some new development ideas and tracking sales of the new release."

"Sales are good, I hope?" She sounded worried, which made him smile. His mother really had no sense of how successful his company had become. This release had launched them to a new level. It was insane, really, how sales were exploding and so far, there had been no bugs or problems like with past releases.

"Things are going really well. Better than ever," he assured her.

"Oh, that's good, dear. I'm glad to hear it. Pass the bread, would you?"

Conversation was easy as they ate and everyone reached for seconds. Susie even took a third helping, laughing as she piled more meatballs onto her plate.

"I can't help it. They're so good and I have to take advantage of being able to eat more than usual while I can."

His mother chuckled. "I'm glad you're enjoying them, dear. I'll pack you up some leftovers to take with you."

Ian turned his attention to Jen. "So, I understand you're a writer. Are you just here to research? Or will you be writing, too?"

"I like to research as I go. I'm hoping to get started with some writing tomorrow, actually," she said.

Ian noticed that a peculiar gleam had come into his mother's eye. She leaned forward and said, "Ian, Jen's new story is set in a software company. It sounds a bit like yours. One of her characters is a software engineer. Maybe she can go into work with you tomorrow and have a look around?"

The request took Ian by surprise and he sat there in silence, considering how that could work.

"Oh, I don't want to be a bother. I know you're very busy." Ian noticed that a flush had crept across Jen's face. That was curious.

"Didn't you mention the other day that you just had a software engineer leave? Maybe Jen can use his office for a week or two. She could write there and do some research, too." She turned to Jen and asked, "How do you research dear? Do you just talk to people?"

Jen smiled. "Yes, a combination of talking to anyone that will talk to me, and using the internet to look things up. Like I said, though, I don't want to get in anyone's way."

Ian couldn't help but notice that she looked excited about the idea and it was starting to grow on him, too. He did have an empty office available and they hadn't even started interviewing yet to fill the position, so the office was going to sit empty for at least a month or two.

"I'd be happy to bring you into work with me. As long as you don't mind staying a full day, you can use the office, and talk to people about what they do and observe. We have weekly status meetings you could sit in on that would give you a feel for what's going on, and daily scrum meetings with the development team."

"Scrum?" Jennifer and his mother said at the same time.

"At RoadRunner Software, we use an Agile development methodology and part of that process is daily scrum meetings. Basically, the first fifteen minutes of the day is a check in on how things are going, any development issues and potential fixes, so we stay on top of everything."

Jen laughed. "It's like you're speaking another language. But it would really be helpful to sit in if you truly don't mind. It will help me give an authentic feeling to the book."

"As long as you don't mind heading in early. I usually aim to be in the office by seven thirty."

"I'm an early riser, normally. That's perfect."

"So, it's all set, then," his mother said happily. She seemed quite pleased with the new arrangement which Ian found amusing. His mother had tried to play match-maker for him many times before and it had never worked. It wouldn't work this time, either, but not for any lack of interest on his part. He and Jen just weren't on the same page about what they wanted. But, maybe if they spent more time together, he could win her over—at least temporarily.

CHAPTER 9

J en woke at six sharp the next morning and took a quick shower to make sure she was ready on time. She'd been surprised by the offer the night before. She'd hoped that at some point she might be able to ask Ian about his work, but this was almost too good to be true. She'd be able to immerse herself in his world and in turn create a more believable story.

The night before at dinner, before Ian had arrived, she'd been thrilled when she met Tim's wife and Susie said she'd read two of her books and loved them. Jen didn't hear that often, as she wasn't that well known of an author, yet. So when she did, it made her day.

She was a little nervous about the day ahead, though. It almost felt like starting a new job. She was waiting in the kitchen with her laptop when Ian came down the stairs from his apartment over the garage.

"Morning. Are you ready to go?" His hair was still damp, but combed neatly into place and she caught a whiff of something that smelled good as he walked by. He was dressed fairly casually, in jeans and a light blue, button-down shirt. Jen knew that software companies were generally more relaxed when it came to dress.

"I'm ready." She followed him out to the BMW and climbed in.

As they drove in, he told her about some of the people in the office, including his assistant, Merry.

"She can help you with whatever you need, and get you set up with the internet in the office. She knows everything."

"Great."

"Oh, and there's plenty of places near the office to get lunch."

"Do you have a favorite?" she asked.

He was quiet for a minute, thinking. "To be honest, I rarely remember to get lunch. Merry sometimes orders me a sandwich if I think of it. There's a place on the corner that's good. Max's Deli."

They rode in comfortable silence the rest of the way and once they were parked and walking into the office, Jen started to feel a bit nervous again. She was anxious to get in and get settled and get started on her writing. She almost didn't mind if she didn't meet many people this first day as she was suddenly feeling shy. Though she enjoyed being around other people and being social, she was more comfortable with small groups and was quite content to work alone for long stretches, and to even go for days at a time with no physical interaction with others. The people in her stories kept her busy, especially when she was in the thick of it.

The office was quiet when they walked in and Jen relaxed a little. Of course it wouldn't be busy yet. It was still early and most people wouldn't be in for close to an hour. Ian gave her a quick tour, and showed her where the small kitchen and coffee machine was.

"Help yourself to coffee or juice or snacks. We keep it all well stocked."

He led her around the corner to a small office with a window looking out over the busy street, and a good-sized gray metal desk and black leather chair.

"My office is at the end of the hall, if you need anything. I'll send Merry in to check on you when she arrives. The scrum meeting is at eight thirty sharp. You'll want to come to that. I'll swing by to get you a few minutes before."

"Thank you." Ian wandered off, and Jen settled at the desk and opened her laptop. She might as well get a sprint or two in before the scrum meeting started. She liked to work in twenty-five minute sprints, or writing sessions, where she turned the internet off and focused on just writing. Writing in chunks like that helped her to stay focused. Once she had the internet up and running, she'd log into the chat room where she met up with a bunch of her writing friends and they did sprints together, taking short breaks in between to chat. Almost like a virtual water cooler. She found that she was much more productive and happier this way, when she was writing with friends. It also made the day fly by.

She started writing and quickly got lost in her story—so much so that she jumped at the sound of a soft knock on her door. A smiling woman with a short, dark brown bob was standing there, looking apologetic.

"I'm so sorry to interrupt. Ian asked me to come by and introduce myself. I'm Merry, his executive assistant. He also asked me to bring you to where the development team sits. They're about to start their morning scrum meeting. He would have brought you, but had to go early to see Cal about an issue."

"Nice to meet you, Merry." Jen put her laptop on pause, and then followed Merry down the hall and around the corner to a large open area. There were very few private offices here. Workstations lined the walls and were scattered in quads around the room. Jen guessed that there were about thirty-five engineers, if that's what everyone in the room did. Ian caught her eye and smiled when Merry led her into the room.

"My desk is just outside of Ian's office, so stop by if you need anything at all," Merry said before she turned and left the room.

Jen stayed in the back of the room and leaned against the side of a desk. Once the room quieted, Ian spoke.

"Morning, everyone. I'll hand this over to Cal in a minute.

First I wanted to introduce you to Jen, who is hiding in the back." He grinned.

"She's a family friend, from the States, and she's a writer. She's going to be working out of this office for the next few weeks and would love to meet many of you and learn more about what you do. She's writing a book set in a software company and we want her to get it right."

There were a bunch of soft laughs, and then he continued. "Cal, it's all yours. Oh, Jen, Cal heads up engineering, and is also a co-founder of the company. You should definitely chat with him at some point."

Cal stood and walked to the center of the room. He looked to be about the same age as Ian, but was a few inches shorter, a few pounds heavier and had a lot less hair. Cal was almost completely bald. But when he smiled and started talking, Jen liked him right away.

"Welcome, Jen. Just to let you know what our scrum meeting is, we're just going over what's going on with development of the products. It helps us to identify where the problems are and to prioritize what needs our attention first."

Jen listened closely, even though she didn't fully understand much of what they were saying when they spoke, specifically about issues with the code. The meeting lasted no more than twenty minutes and then everyone went back to their desks.

AFTER THE MEETING, CAL FOLLOWED IAN INTO HIS OFFICE AND shut the door behind him. Ian settled into his chair and leaned back, waiting for Cal to ask whatever it was he needed to know.

"So, what's the deal with Jen? Why is she really here? Is there something going on between the two of you?"

Ian didn't blame him for asking the question. It was out of the ordinary for him to bring someone in to just observe them, especially a pretty young woman who also happened to be living with him, sort of.

"It's not like that," he said simply.

Cal raised his eyebrows. "Why not? She's hot and seems smart. Perfect for you, maybe?"

"She is hot. But she doesn't do casual. I don't do serious."

Cal just stared at him, then shook his head and said, "You're an idiot, you do know that?"

Ian smiled. "It's complicated."

"No, it's not. Why can't you just date like a normal person? No one ever knows if something is going to be serious until it goes there. Why not just enjoy yourselves and see what happens?" He grinned. "Look how happy Jane and I are. Who would have thought that a one-night stand would turn into anything more, let alone marriage? You never do know."

"Oh, I agree. I'd be up for a fling, but she isn't. She's only here for a few months and then goes back to the States, and she's living at my mother's house. It's a little too close for comfort."

"Your mother wouldn't approve?"

"Of a fling under her roof? No, I don't think so. Though she would love to see me married off again."

"Hmmm. Well, you're only there for a few weeks right? You should be back in your condo soon. Be her friend, see where it goes…but you're crazy if you don't at least try."

"Are you done?" Ian asked. Cal was recently married and now he wanted all of his friends to join him on the other side. Ian was happy for him. But, he wasn't eager to get married again anytime soon…to anyone.

"Yeah, I'm done. She just seems like a nice girl."

Ian chuckled. "She is. In fact, why don't you stop by her office and talk to her. She wants to learn more about what software engineers do. You can fill her in on your job and answer any questions she might have."

"Okay, I'll do that."

Cal left and Ian pulled up his email and started going through it. Cal's words kept interrupting his thoughts, though. Even if Jen didn't want to date him, they could at least be friends. He could show her around a bit and they could spend some time together. She didn't know anyone in Ireland besides his family, so she could use a friend. Tim was busy with Susie who was about to give birth any day, so it was practically his responsibility to show her a good time. That decided, he turned his attention back to his email.

JEN HAD JOTTED DOWN AS MANY NOTES AS POSSIBLE AND ONCE she was back at her desk, she typed it into her research doc and made a note to look up anything that wasn't clear. She was just finishing up when there was a knock at her door. She looked up and saw Ian's friend Cal standing in the doorway.

"Ian said you're writing a book about a software engineer and I need to talk to you."

Jen laughed. "You're the CTO, right?"

"That's right. I'm the head geek, all things tech. I started out writing code as a regular staff engineer when we were right out of school. Ian and I worked at the same company."

"I'd love to learn more about what you do, what it's like working at a company like this."

"Well, I'm your man" He settled into the chair across from her desk and leaned back. "Ask me anything."

Jen picked up her pen and grabbed her note pad. For the next half hour she peppered him with questions, asking about a typical day, and what he actually did and how it fit into what the others did. Cal explained it all so well that Jen was racing to capture everything on paper as best she could. Finally, they wrapped up.

"I can't thank you enough. I might double-check some of this or have more questions, if that's all right?"

"Of course. Use me as much as you can while you're here." He grinned. "It's a nice break for me."

"I really do appreciate it." She was thrilled. She never would have learned half of what Cal told her by googling. There was nothing like real research.

Cal stood up and started to walk toward the door, then he turned back and casually said, "So, what do you think about

Ian? You two should hang out while he's staying at his mother's place."

His question caught her off guard. "Ian's great, but he's very busy. He works a lot."

Cal frowned. "He works too much. I agree with you. We need to do something about that."

"I don't know if you can change people. It's who they are. My last boyfriend was the same way, a workaholic. That's why he's my ex."

Cal pushed the door open. "Right. Well, I'll let you get back to your work and it's time for me to do the same. Nice talking to you, Jen."

He left and shut the door behind him, and Jen sighed. Cal had been anything but subtle and she was flattered that he thought she might be someone Ian should date. Too bad that wasn't going to happen.

CHAPTER 10

J en leaned back in her chair and rubbed her eyes. The glare from the sun on her computer was getting worse and her neck was feeling stiff from being hunched over her desk in the same position for so long. She usually avoided that by getting up every half hour or so to walk around. But today, she lost herself in her story instead. She got up to stretch and close the blinds a bit. The morning had flown by and a quick glance at the time confirmed that it was nearly noon. She turned at the sound of a light knock on her door and then Merry came in.

"Do you have lunch plans?" she asked. Jen's stomach grumbled in response.

"No. I am getting hungry, though."

"Let's go around the corner and grab a sandwich. There's a good deli there. I'm going to bring something back for Ian."

"Oh, that's nice of you." Jen grabbed her purse and followed Merry down the hall.

Merry chuckled. "If I don't bring him food, he won't eat. He never goes out to lunch. He's always glued to his computer. Even when I bring it, he sometimes doesn't touch it for hours."

She led them outside and a few minutes later they arrived at Max's Deli. Jen remembered Ian had mentioned the name. The place was packed.

"Everything here is good, but the chicken club sandwiches are amazing," Merry said.

Jen ordered one and Merry got two sandwiches, one for her and one to bring back for Ian. They found a small table in the back of the room and settled in to eat.

Jen learned that Merry was married to her high school sweetheart and that they had no children, just four cats that they spoiled terribly.

"What about you? Any boyfriend missing you back home?" Merry asked.

Jen chuckled. "No. Completely single. I broke up with someone a few weeks ago."

"Oh, I'm sorry to hear it." She looked sympathetic and added, "I'm sure it's for the best, though, right? Or maybe you'll get back together when you go home?"

Jen shook her head. "No, we will most definitely not be getting back together." She told Merry all about Paul and his workaholic ways.

"He sounds like someone we know," Merry said with a smile. "I think it's more of a habit, though, with Ian. I'm pretty sure he could work less hours if he wanted to. We're past the start-up phase now, and he has good people working for him. I keep telling him he needs to take a vacation, even if he doesn't actually go anywhere."

"We call that a stay-cation where I'm from. It's nice to just stay home and do nothing sometimes."

"I'm not sure if Ian is capable of that. I'd like to see him try, though."

"Do you often have to work late, too?" Jen asked.

"No, not usually. He's good about that. Ian usually leaves at a decent hour. But I think he goes home and goes back to work. He sends me emails at all hours, but I don't usually do anything with them until the morning."

"Have you met his daughter?" Jen was curious about his little girl.

"Ella? Yes, he brings her by occasionally. She's a sweet

thing. Full of energy." She paused for a minute then added, "His ex-wife is a different story, though."

"You've met her, too?"

"Just once, but that was enough. It was when we first started the company and they were getting divorced. She waltzed in with her attorney and demanded a tour. She had no interest in visiting before that. I don't think she liked me very much."

"Really? Why do you say that?"

"I saw her husband more than she did. She didn't understand it, or trust me."

"But you were married then, right?"

"Yes, but I don't think that mattered much to her. She was an odd one. We were all happy when their divorce was finalized, though I know it was hard on Ian. The company hit it big a year later. That's when all the other women started chasing him."

"Really? He mentioned that he doesn't date much."

"He got burned a few times. Fell hard and found out they were more interested in his bank account. He is more cautious now. Doesn't get close to people too soon. I don't blame him."

"I don't either. Did his ex-wife remarry?" Jen wondered.

"She did, almost immediately, after they divorced. She married well, too, to an older fellow with a lovely home in the country.

"That sounds nice."

"I don't think he's quite the catch she thought though. Ian said she's gone back to work part-time."

"Maybe she enjoys working?" Jen couldn't imagine just sitting around doing nothing.

Merry laughed. "You'll meet her, I'm sure. I almost feel sorry for her. Almost." She stood up and gathered her trash to throw out. Jen did the same.

"You must think I'm such a bitch," Merry said. "Here I am going on and on about Ian's ex-wife. I probably shouldn't have done that. But it was just so nice to have lunch with another girl. You probably noticed there's very few of us there."

"I did notice that, and I don't think you're a bitch at all. I think we're going to get along great."

When they were back in the building and just outside Jen's office, Merry said, "If you want to stretch your legs later this afternoon, I usually take a walk up the street for a coffee."

"Oh, that sounds perfect. I usually start to fade around two."

BEFORE SHE KNEW IT, THE DAY WAS OVER. JEN HEARD IAN saying goodbye to Merry and then he was standing in the door way. Was it half past five already? Jen had managed to finish several chapters, and was deep in the middle of another and had lost all track of time.

"Are you about ready to go?" he asked.

"Yes, I'm just shutting down. I'm ready. She gathered up her notebook, laptop and charger and stuffed them into her tote bag.

On the drive home, Ian asked her about her day and as she started to answer, his phone rang and he spent almost the entire ride talking to someone in sales named Ben about what sounded like a major issue with one of their key accounts. He sounded agitated and stressed out, and the feeling was conta-gious. He finally ended the call as they pulled onto his mother's street.

"I'm sorry about that. I know it was rude of me. We just have a situation going on that we're trying to figure out. Ben and I needed to talk before this client comes in tomorrow to sit down with us. Jim MacMurray is the owner of the company. He's thinking about switching to a different vendor and wants us to give him a good reason not to." He grinned. "Tomorrow is going to be a long day. Wish me luck."

"Good luck. Is there anything I can do to help?" She couldn't imagine what it would be, but wished there was some-thing she could do.

"Thanks. If you don't mind getting up a little earlier tomorrow, I could use the extra time to get ready."

Jen smiled. "I can do that."

Aunt Sorcha was stirring something on the stove and looked up when she heard them walk in.

"Hello to both of you. Did you have a good day? Dinner should be ready in about an hour."

The delicious scent of butter, garlic and basil filled the room. But it was lost on Ian.

"Don't wait for me on dinner. I have some work to do. I'll come down later and find something."

"Okay, dear, if you're sure." She turned to Jen. "I hope you're hungry."

"I'm always hungry," Jen said with a smile. "What are you making? It smells amazing."

"It's just a chicken and mushroom risotto. That's how I use up leftovers." She looked pleased at the compliment.

"Can I do anything to help?"

She thought for a minute. "Why don't you slice up those tomatoes for the salad? And tell me about your day. I want to hear all about it."

After a relaxing dinner, they watched television for a while. Jen had planned to read over what she'd written earlier in the day, but her eyes grew heavy early and she went off to bed instead. Aunt Sorcha was right. It did take a few days to adjust fully to the time difference, plus she'd been up early to head into the office. As soon as her head touched the pillow, she fell fast asleep.

CHAPTER 11

Tension was thick in the office the next morning. Jen could sense it as she walked to the kitchen to make a coffee around ten. Instead of the joking and laughing that had filled the halls the day before, there was an eerie silence. Ian had barely spoken on the drive in and she was too sleepy to talk so it was fine by her. Merry looked up and smiled when she walked by her desk. Jen stopped for a moment and glanced around to make sure no one could over hear her.

"You can hear a pin drop in here. Is this meeting really that big of a deal?"

"With Jim MacMurray? Yes, it's huge. He just acquired another company and needs to decide if he's going to use our software for the entire organization and all their clients. It would be their biggest deal yet."

"Oh. Now I'm going to worry, too. I'll just head back to my office and stay out of the way."

Merry chuckled. "Just think good thoughts. They'll need them. Ian said they are on the fence between us and one other company."

Jen settled back at her desk and quickly got lost in her story world. She was finishing up a scene and racing to get the words down as quickly as they came to her. That's always how it was when the story was flowing and she was just trying to keep up.

She much preferred it to when she sat struggling to figure out what needed to happen next and it felt more like pulling teeth to get any words down at all.

She reached for a sip of her coffee and was dismayed but not terribly surprised to find that it was stone cold. She'd forgotten all about it and it had sat there for at least thirty minutes. There was a microwave in the kitchen, though, so she could go heat it up and give her legs a stretch. She knew that sitting for hours on end was not at all good for the body and she hated that crunchy feeling her muscles got when she waited too long.

The kitchen was empty, so she popped her coffee in the microwave and waited for it to heat up. An older gentleman that she didn't recognize walked in, and she smiled and introduced herself.

"Hello, I don't think we've met yet. I'm Jen."

The older man held out his hand. "I'm Jim, pleasure to meet you. What do you do here, Jen?"

She was wondering the same thing about him. She didn't remember seeing him the day before. He was a lot older than most of the other employees. His hair was snow white and he looked to be in his early sixties.

"I don't actually work here. I'm just riding in with Ian for a few weeks, or as long as he'll put up with me, I suppose. I'm staying with his family for a few months and working on a new book."

He looked confused, so she continued to explain. "His Aunt Sorcha suggested I work out of an empty office here and do research at the same time, so I'll be chatting with people about what they do. That way, I won't make too many mistakes in my book."

He seemed intrigued. "Are you writing fiction or non-fiction?"

"Fiction. I write romance novels, actually."

He smiled at that. "You do? That's splendid! My wife can't get enough of them. I wonder if she's read any of yours?"

"I doubt it. I'm not that well known." She grinned and added, "yet!"

"That's the right attitude." He checked his watch and said, "I'm actually early for a meeting and have about fifteen minutes to kill if you want to ask me some questions. I'd be happy to help and the wife would get a kick out of this."

"You don't mind? That would be super. My office is just down the hall."

She led him into her office and he settled himself in the chair across from her desk. She picked up her pen and paper and prepared to take notes.

"So, what is your role?"

He leaned back and thought for a moment before speaking.

"It's changed a bit over the years. I started out in software engineering, of course, like everyone in this industry does, I think. But I've always liked people interaction, so I moved into the implementation side of things, where I'd connect the client's software with ours. Then I moved into the architect role, where I'd meet with the clients first and scope out what they wanted to have done and the plan for the engineers to handle the integration. After that, I started leading small teams and then bigger ones. Then eventually headed up the Professional Services team and we started taking on even huge multi-year consulting projects."

Jen looked up from her note-taking. "I didn't realize that Ian's company did that?"

"Did what?" Jim asked.

"Huge projects like that, or that they had a consulting division."

"I don't think they do. They usually work through a company like mine for those types of projects."

"A company like yours?" Jen repeated, feeling as though she'd missed something.

"Yes, MacMurray Consulting. I'm Jim MacMurray. Not sure if I mentioned my last name earlier. Sorry about that."

"Oh, well…" Jen stammered, feeling like a complete idiot. Merry walked by at that moment and did a double-take as she saw who was sitting in Jen's office. She looked both puzzled and relieved to see him.

"Mr. MacMurray, it's so nice to see you again. May I show you to the conference room? The team is waiting there for you."

He stood and held his hand out again to Jen. "It was lovely chatting with you my dear. What did you say your last name was?

"Graham."

"Graham, Jennifer Graham. All right, then. I'll run that by the wife. If she hasn't read you yet, I'll tell her she must."

Jen smiled. He didn't seem intimidating at all. Mr. MacMurray seemed like a very sweet man.

"That's very nice of you. Thank you for chatting with me. It was very helpful."

"If you have any other questions, young lady, you just give me a holler." He reached into his pocket, opened his wallet, and handed her a business card.

Merry whisked him away, and then returned few minutes later and shut the door behind her.

"How on earth did you end up bringing Jim MacMurray into your office? He's always early and we were starting to worry."

"I had no idea that's who it was. I ran into him in the kitchen and we started talking. I thought he worked here."

Merry giggled at the thought of it. "Ian would flip if he knew what you'd been up to. At least he seemed to be in a good mood. Maybe it will turn out to be a good thing."

―――――

JEN DIDN'T SEE IAN UNTIL THE END OF THE DAY WHEN IT WAS time to go. He was quiet as they got into the car and didn't say much until they were a few minutes down the road.

"You seemed to make quite an impression on Jim MacMurray."

"I thought he was just a nice older guy that worked for you. He offered to answer questions for me."

Ian chuckled. "I'm not upset in the least. If anything, you warmed him up for us. I've never seen him in such a good mood. The meeting went about as well as it possibly could have."

"You closed the deal?! That's great." Jen was happy for him.

"Not quite yet. These things happen in stages. He's meeting with our competition next week. We'll know more after that."

"Oh. Well, I hope it works out."

"I'm optimistic. We made our best case. That's all we can do."

"I'll keep my fingers crossed for you." Jen stared out the window at the traffic. It was hard to believe tomorrow was Friday already. "Do you have your daughter this weekend?" She wondered if it might be his weekend and was curious to meet Ella.

"I do. We'll leave the office early tomorrow. I usually meet her mother at four, halfway between her house and mine."

"I look forward to meeting her."

Ian chuckled. "She's curious to meet you, too. I told her that a famous lady author is staying with us."

"Hardly famous," she demurred.

"Think positive. You could be one day."

"That would be nice. I'm happy enough, though. I love what I do, and thankfully enough people like it that I get to keep doing it."

"See, you're on your way to world domination," he teased.

"Are you working tonight?" she asked.

"I hadn't really thought about it. I guess I usually do, though," he said. "Why do you ask? Did you want to do something?"

"Merry mentioned that she and her husband and a bunch of the engineers, including Cal and his wife, were all going to meet up at that pub we went to the other night. It sounded like it could be fun. I told her I wasn't sure if I could make it, but I'd check with you."

He hesitated for just a moment, then said, "Sure, that could be fun, and I'm sure you're dying to get out."

"I wouldn't mind going out for a little while," she admitted.

Ian pulled into the driveway and shut off the engine. Jen noticed that Aunt Sorcha's car wasn't there and remembered she'd said something about going out with her friends.

"It's her bingo night. Big night out," Ian said with a grin as they walked inside. "Want to go in about a half-hour?"

CHAPTER 12

"When was the last time you went on holiday?" Cal asked. Ian ignored the question. They'd been at the bar for just over an hour. It was packed, but it was always busy at MacGregor's, and it was a Thursday night. A two-man band played soft rock in a corner, while two bartenders ran non-stop from one customer to the next.

Jen seemed to be having a good time. She was busy chatting with Merry and her husband, a few stools down. Jen looked great tonight. She'd changed from what she was wearing earlier in the day, trading gray pants and a baby blue sweater for jeans and a white silky top. The hair that had been pulled back all day in a ponytail was now down and fell past her shoulders in sleek, shiny waves.

"Earth to Ian. Did you hear what I just asked you?" Cal demanded his attention.

"Sorry, what was that?"

"I asked when you last took time off." Cal leaned against the bar and stared at him intently, waiting for a reply.

Ian sighed. He knew Cal had a point. It had been too long since he'd taken any time off. He was way overdue.

"It's been a while," he admitted. He took a long sip of his beer, hoping Cal would drop it and change the subject. No such luck, and he noticed Jen inching closer. It was obvious that she'd heard this last exchange.

"It's a good time right now. The release is out and going strong. Nothing else urgent is pending. We can more than cover for you if you want to take a week off soon and go relax. Go to a Caribbean Island or just stay home and do nothing."

"I don't know. Maybe after the MacMurray deal is finalized I'll think about it."

"Do you think he'll decide to go with you? He seemed like such a sweet guy," Jen asked. Ian still couldn't get over the fact that his biggest client had somehow wandered into Jen's office for a chat.

He chuckled. "Sweet isn't how I would think to describe Jim MacMurray."

"No, he really was lovely," Jen insisted.

MacMurray most certainly was not lovely. Jen was, though. There was a fresh sweetness about her that was very appealing. Freckles dusted the tip of her nose and ran across her cheeks. Her eyes were big and dark and he had to force himself not to stare into them. It didn't help to shift his gaze to her lips. They were a dusty pink and slightly full, plumped for kissing. And he couldn't go there.

He could have sworn that he got the sense that Jen was attracted to him the first night that they met. But once they had the conversation, he hadn't felt that vibe since. Jen had put him firmly into the friend box. And he wasn't liking it. Not one bit. He wasn't looking for a relationship, but he really would enjoy a fling. Yes, a fling would be perfect.

But she wasn't paying much attention to him at all, and truth be told, he wasn't used to that. Since his company had gone public, he had been covered quite a bit in the local papers. As soon as women found out who he was, they were generally interested in whatever he had to offer.

He was always completely up front with them of course, which if anything seemed to make them even more interested. He knew that more than one of them saw that as a challenge and were sure that they could be the one to tame him, and ultimately to marry.

He watched for the signs, though, and as soon as he sensed that the woman he was currently dating might be getting ideas along those lines, he usually ended things. As nicely as he could. There really hadn't been many women that he wanted to go out with more than a couple of times, anyway, so it wasn't often an issue.

Maybe he would go on holiday soon. It would make Cal happy, and as much as he hated to admit it, his best friend was right.

"You look deep in thought. I hope it's not a work problem?" Jen asked. She was by his side now, waiting for the bartender to return with a fresh pint.

Ian chuckled. "No, not at all." He finished the last sip of beer in his mug and set it on the bar. Simon, the bartender, handed Jen her new beer and glanced at Ian's empty mug. Ian nodded to the unspoken question and Simon quickly poured him a fresh draft as well. Drink in hand, he tapped his mug against Jen's.

"Cheers!"

"Cheers. What are we cheering to?" Jen asked with a smile.

"I'm thinking about taking some time off."

"Oh, that's wonderful. Will you go somewhere?"

"Maybe, maybe not. I think I'll just play it by ear." He took a sip of his beer and then smiled at her. "Maybe I'll take you sight-seeing, and play tourist. We could see things you won't find on any list of popular attractions."

She looked intrigued. "Like what?"

"Castles in the countryside, tiny pubs in villages far away from here. Life outside Dublin."

Her eyes lit up. "I'd love to see that."

"Your hair looks pretty down like that."

The shift in conversation threw her off balance. Was that a slight blush he saw on her cheeks? Interesting.

"Thanks. I just wear it up when I'm working to keep it out of my way, so I can focus."

"It looks cute up, too."

"You're flirting," she accused him as she reached for her beer.

"Maybe a little," he admitted. "Is that a bad thing?"

Jen sighed. "We talked about this not being a good idea."

"True. We did. I thought it was a good idea. You didn't. Maybe I was hoping you'd change your mind."

The blush on her cheeks deepened. He knew he was having an effect on her.

"I haven't changed my mind," she finally said.

"Pity. So let's change the subject. Tell me about the book you're writing?"

Her eyes narrowed. "You really want to know?"

"Yes, I do. You seem surprised. I take it your ex wasn't all that interested in your books?"

"No, not really. He was interested in the law, that was about it."

"So tell me about them." He was curious to learn more about her. What she wrote about could give him insight into who she was.

"Well, they're romances. Big, soapy sagas that show the struggles people go through to find love."

"And do they?"

"Do they what?"

"Find love?"

She laughed. "Of course they do. Otherwise they wouldn't be considered a romance. A happy ending is a must."

"I love a good happy ending," he said as he finished his drink.

"I wouldn't have taken you for a romance reader."

"I'm not. But my favorite stories always end well."

"So, you're an optimist?" She sounded pleased.

"I suppose I am." He looked around the bar. The crowd was emptying out

"I'll see you guys in the morning," Cal called out as he and his wife headed for the door. Merry and her husband were right behind them.

"Do you want to stay or should we head out soon?" he asked.

"We should probably go, too," Jen said. Ian wasn't sure, but he thought there was a hint of reluctance in her voice, or maybe it was just wishful thinking on his part.

Ian grabbed the bill and waved Jen's money away when she tried to hand it to him.

"I can buy you a few drinks."

Ten minutes later they were home and the house was dark and quiet, except for a light over the kitchen stove that his mother had left on.

Ian was about to turn to the stairs and go up to his apartment when Jen lightly touched his arm.

"Thank you for tonight. That was fun. I really like your friends, the people you work with." Her voice was soft and sweet and he acted quickly before he lost his nerve. He grabbed both of her wrists and pulled her toward him. The quick intake of breath told him that he'd caught her by surprise and that she liked it.

"I'm glad you had fun." He paused for a moment and lightly stroked the soft skin on her inside wrists. She looked up at him, her eyes wide and sweet, and he lost his nerve. Came to his senses was more like it. He wanted nothing more than to crush his lips down onto hers, but knew it would be taking advantage and that she'd probably regret it. The timing wasn't right. Not until he was certain it was what she really wanted. He released her hands and stepped back. He saw confusion cloud her eyes and was glad he'd hesitated.

"Good night. See you bright and early tomorrow?" he asked.

"Yes, of course. Good night."

CHAPTER 13

Ian disappeared up the stairs to his apartment and Jen watched him go, a little confused and relieved at the same time. They'd almost kissed. She was sure of it, and at that moment, she'd wanted it to happen. When Ian touched her, her senses went haywire. She'd never had such a strong physical reaction to anyone before. She could only imagine what it would be like if they kissed. It definitely wouldn't be casual. Not for her anyway, so she was grateful that he'd taken a step back.

When she walked into the kitchen the next morning, Ian was waiting for her and chatting with Aunt Sorcha. She was relieved to see that there was no awkwardness, but knew there might have been if they'd kissed. He smiled when he saw her and gave his mother a kiss goodbye.

"We'll be back early today after we pick up Ella," he reminded her as they left.

Once they climbed into his car and and made their way into traffic, Ian spoke.

"So that was a fun time last night." He fiddled with the radio station, trying several until he found a song he liked.

"Yes, it was."

"Do you mind riding with me after work to pick up Ella? It

will be easiest if we head straight out there from the office instead of going home to my mother's first. It's in the opposite direction."

"Oh, that's fine."

"I'll apologize in advance for Nadine. She's likely to be bitchy and she'll never believe that we're just friends."

Jen wasn't sure she blamed her. She'd probably think the same if Ian was her ex and showed up with a strange woman in tow to collect his daughter.

"Well, we are. So, she can believe it or not. It doesn't matter a bit to me."

He shot her a quick sideways look, then turned his attention back to the road.

"All right, then."

IAN DISAPPEARED INTO HIS OFFICE ONCE THEY ARRIVED AND JEN did the same, stopping only when Merry walked by on her way to her desk and came in to chat first.

"That was so much fun last night. We need to do that more often. I miss going out after work. It's usually just the guys, so I very rarely join them. You need to stick around here as long as possible."

Jen laughed. "I guess it depends how soon they fill this role and need the office back?"

"They haven't even started to interview yet, so it will be a while."

"Oh. Well, that's good, then." Jen had to admit, she was enjoying coming into the office and being around people. She was still able to close her office door if she needed to focus, so it was the best of both worlds.

"It was nice to see Ian getting out more, too. Twice in one week. You're a good influence on him."

"I don't know about that." Was she a good influence? Or more of a distraction?

Merry glanced at her watch. "Well, I wish I could stay and

chat, but it's time for me to settle in and do a little work. Did you bring lunch in today?"

Jen shook her head. She hadn't even thought to.

"Good. We'll go grab a bite somewhere."

She left and Jen opened her laptop. The rest of the day raced by. She attended the morning scrum meeting, and one of the software engineers showed her what he was working on and gave her a five minute lesson in writing code. It was like a foreign language. She asked the engineer, Travis, if he enjoyed the work. His eyes lit up.

"I love it. I started taking things apart when I was a kid and then got hooked on video games. Being a software engineer is the ultimate game. It's like a big puzzle that you are continually solving and adapting to make the software do different things."

Jen thought about that analogy and made some notes immediately after their conversation, so she wouldn't forget. She had never been interested in video games, but she could see how what he did was similar to a giant puzzle. She much preferred to build things with words instead of code, but she supposed that creating a story was a puzzle too, in a way, figuring out all the pieces and how to weave it all together.

Lunch with Merry was fun, and she got a lot of solid writing done in the afternoon, even though it was a shorter day than usual. She kept an eye on the time, and at three thirty, started to wrap things up. Ian came by a few minutes later, and they were on their way.

His phone rang non-stop as they drove and Jen stared out the window at traffic while semi-listening to him discuss various goings on at the company. She paid closer attention, though, when she heard him mention Jim MacMurray.

"MacMurray let us know he may not be making a decision for another week or two. I don't know if that means he's considering additional vendors. I know he's meeting with one other this week. I know, nothing we can do at this point except wait." Ian was quiet while whoever was on the other line talked and then he chuckled.

"You know I'm not good at being patient. Right. Talk to

you tomorrow. What? That's fantastic news. Congrats! Tell Jane I said the same." Ian ended the call as he turned off the highway.

"Cal's pregnant. Rather, his wife, Jane is. They just found out."

"Oh, that's wonderful news! Their first?"

"Yeah. They've been trying for a while. He told me, but they're not saying anything publicly for a few months, until it's safe to say it."

"That makes sense."

A few minutes later, Ian pulled into the driveway of a large white house with a huge porch and a Mercedes sedan in the driveway. When he turned off the engine, the front door opened and a small girl ran out onto the lawn, followed by a pretty, dark-haired woman that Jen assumed must be Ian's ex-wife. He opened his door and Jen did the same.

"Daddy!" She ran over and threw her arms around Ian. He lifted her up high and gave her a loud kiss.

"How's my princess? Have you been a good girl this week?"

"Of course!" Ella squirmed to get down. Ian set her down just as Nadine reached them. She was holding Ella's pink backpack and handed it over to Ian. She looked at Jen curiously.

"You must be the writer? The one staying with Ian's mother? I wonder if I've heard of you?" The way she said the word writer made it sound like something dubious.

Jen smiled and held out her hand. "I doubt it. I'm not well known. I write romance as Jennifer Graham."

Nadine wrinkled her nose. "I didn't realize you wrote romance. I don't read that kind of thing."

Of course she didn't. Jen was used to getting that kind of response, though, when people learned what kind of books she wrote.

"That's too bad. Fortunately, lots of people do, though, or I'd be out of a job," she said sweetly.

"Jen's actually been coming into work with me and using one of our empty offices to write in," Ian added.

"Really? Can't you just write at home?" Jen noticed with

curiosity that Nadine didn't seem to like the idea of Jen going into Ian's office.

"The book she is working on is set in a software company," Ian explained.

Nadine changed the subject. "What time is good for you on Sunday? I can swing by and get her as I'll be heading that way."

"How's three or so?"

"I'll see you at three. Bye, Ella. Give me a kiss goodbye." Ella threw her arms around her mother's neck, gave her a quick kiss, then ran to the BMW and tried to open the door on Ian's side.

"Hold on, dear. I'll be right there," he said.

Ian let her in, buckled her into the car seat and once they were all settled, they set off.

Ella chattered non-stop for about ten minutes, then grew totally silent. Jen turned around to check on her and saw that she was fast asleep.

"She's out?" Ian asked.

"Completely."

"Happens almost every time. She'll get a good nap in and then be wide awake when we reach the house. She's always so excited to see my mother, and the feeling is mutual."

Ella slowly woke up when they arrived home, and Jen got out of the car and shut the door. Aunt Sorcha's car was gone, but Jen imagined she'd be home shortly. She watched as Ian unbuckled Ella and then the little girl raced over to Jen, holding a pink soccer ball.

"Will you play with me?" she pleaded.

"Sure. Let me set my bag down and I'll be right there." Jen opened the front door and tossed her bag inside. Ian did the same with Ella's pink backpack. His phone rang again and he answered it as Jen made her way over to Ella. She was kicking the ball around the yard and clapped her hands when she saw Jen. They kicked the ball back and forth while Ian sat on the front step, glued to his phone.

Jen assumed he'd finish the call and join them, but he

didn't. Once he ended the call, he started checking email. And Jen started to fume. She didn't mind playing with Ella, but was annoyed that he was just sitting there. He could have easily joined them. She finally motioned for him to join them and he called out, "I'll be there in a few minutes."

Fifteen minutes later, he was still sitting there, texting away. Ella seemed like she was tiring. Jen was annoyed.

"Ella, I have to run inside for a minute. Your daddy will come and play with you now." She said it loudly enough that Ian heard her and she glared at him as she walked past him and into the house.

"Go play with your daughter," she said. Her tone was cold and he looked up at her in surprise. He put the phone down though and got up to go to Ella.

Jen brought her bag up to her room and glanced out the window. Ian and Ella were running around with the ball and Aunt Sorcha was pulling into the driveway. Her initial take on Ian was unfortunately correct. He was too much like Paul. If she hadn't been there, would he have played with Ella or sat there on the phone while she chased the ball around by herself?

Jen came out of her room just as Aunt Sorcha was coming into the kitchen carrying a large bag of groceries.

"Can I help?" Jen offered.

"Sure. There's another two bags in the car, dear, if you wouldn't mind grabbing them."

Jen went outside to get the bags and neither Ella or Ian looked her way, they were so intent on their game. She was glad to see it. She brought the groceries into the kitchen and helped Aunt Sorcha unload everything and put it all away.

"Ian is taking Ella to her favorite restaurant for dinner tonight. He said you're welcome to go with them, if you like, or I'd love to have you join me and the girls for bingo and then a bite to eat after."

Jen smiled. It was an easy decision. "I'd love to join you for bingo. Ian and Ella can enjoy some quality father-daughter time together."

Aunt Sorcha looked pleased to hear it. "Excellent. We'll leave in twenty minutes."

CHAPTER 14

As Jen and Aunt Sorcha walked out the front door, Ian and Ella were heading toward them.

"Off to bingo, then?" Ian looked amused.

"I love bingo," Jen said.

Ian raised his eyebrows and opened his mouth to say something, but then Ella tugged on his arm and he just shook his head instead.

"Have a nice dinner, you two," Aunt Sorcha said as she walked past them and Jen followed close behind.

The community center was a short drive away and when they arrived, Gracie was already there and had two seats saved for them. Aunt Sorcha led Jen over to the sign-in desk, where they paid for their bingo sheets and Jen got a purple dabber to mark her spots.

"Is Frank coming?" Gracie asked as they settled next to her at the table.

"I haven't seen him this week. He usually comes, though."

"I saved a seat for him. Unless he comes with that Lindy O'Shea, then there won't be room."

Aunt Sorcha shot her a look of surprise. "Why would he come with Lindy?"

"Well, Betty said that Lindy was asking about Frank and mentioned how much she likes bingo."

"Hmmm. Well, she doesn't waste any time, does she?"

"Who is Lindy?" Jen asked, curious why the mention of her name seemed to ruffle Aunt Sorcha's feathers.

"She's new in town. Moved here a few months ago after her divorce was finalized. She lives in a condo." Jen chuckled. Aunt Sorcha made it sound like a dirty word.

"I live in a condo," she said with a laugh.

"Oh, I'm sure yours is lovely. Lindy is just—she's just so obviously looking for a man."

"That's hardly a crime," Gracie said. "And Frank is single. It's about time he started dating. Could be perfect timing for him."

Aunt Sorcha scowled and Jen tried not to smile but couldn't help it when a few minutes later, Frank arrived and settled into the empty seat next to Aunt Sorcha. Lindy was nowhere to be seen.

"Hello, ladies. Jennifer is it? Nice to see you again." He exchanged hellos with the other two and then went to get his bingo card and dabber.

The games began five minutes later and Jen had to pay attention to keep up. Some of these ladies were playing multiple bingo cards and she didn't know how they did it. She had all she could do to manage one. They played for an hour and a half and both Aunt Sorcha and Gracie each won a round, which gave them both a hundred Euros.

"Looks like dinner is on us," Gracie said as they left the bingo hall and walked to the pub just down the street. Frank joined them and they'd just settled at a table in the restaurant when an older woman with fluffy, blonde hair that was sprayed into a bob that just reached her jaw and moved in one stiff piece when she spoke, headed their way.

"Oh, hello, everyone." She walked over to their table, holding a glass of white wine, and smiled at Frank.

"I'm sorry I didn't make it to bingo. It would have been fun to play with you all. I hope you don't mind if I join you?" She didn't wait for an answer, just walked over to the empty seat next to Frank and sat down.

"It's so good to see you." She smiled right at Frank and he looked a bit flustered. Then she briefly glanced around the table. "Great to see all of you." She frowned when she saw Jen and then held out her hand. "I don't think we've met. I'm Lindy."

Jen shook her hand and couldn't help noticing how smooth her skin was and how perfectly polished her nails, as if she'd just had a manicure. Aunt Sorcha did not look pleased with the new arrival.

"Sorcha, what would you like to drink? I think I'm going to splurge and have a glass of wine," Gracie said.

"Wine? I think I'll join you."

"Really? I don't remember the last time you had wine." Gracie sounded surprised.

"I like a glass every now and then. Jen probably will, too?"

"Sure, I rarely say no to wine."

They ordered their drinks when the waitress came by, and also decided to share a few pizzas. Lindy mostly spoke to Frank and ignored the rest of them. Jen watched it all with interest. Lindy's flirting with Frank was so blatant. She was laughing and lightly touching his arm every now and then. He didn't seem to mind the attention, though if Jen had to guess, she would bet he was somewhat clueless as to her intentions. One glance at Aunt Sorcha told her that she was very much aware of what Lindy was up to and that she didn't like it a bit. Which was also interesting. Maybe this would be the push Aunt Sorcha needed to dip her toes back into the dating pool.

The pizza was delicious and there wasn't one slice left when the waitress came to clear their plates. They all passed on dessert but did order hot tea all around. Jen was stirring a bit of sugar into hers when she overheard Lindy say something that almost made her drop her spoon.

"Frank, I know it's a bit forward to ask, but I happen to have two tickets to a charity ball Saturday night and I'd love it so much if you could come with me."

He looked at her in shock and she quickly added, "You'd

be doing me a huge favor, actually, as my sister was supposed to go with me, but can't make it."

The table grew so quiet that you could have heard a pin drop. All eyes were on Frank, waiting for his reply. He glanced around the table nervously. Lindy put her hand on his arm and batted her fake eyelashes at him.

"You don't have plans already, do you?"

"Well, no. I don't," he stammered.

Lindy beamed and then went in for the close. "We'll have so much fun! Have you been before?"

He shook his head.

"So, it's settled, then! I'm so excited to go with you."

Frank glanced around the table in confusion. He never actually did say yes, but that hadn't stopped Lindy. Now, in order not to go, he would have to come out and say no. Jen could see small beads of sweat on his brow and knew that wasn't likely to happen.

Lindy smiled and looked at Aunt Sorcha, and in a sugary sweet tone asked, "Are you dating anyone these days, Sorcha? I don't think I've ever heard you mention it."

Aunt Sorcha was quiet for a moment and then said, "Peter Thompson actually asked me to go to dinner last week."

Lindy gasped. "Peter Thompson? Of Thompson Motors?"

Aunt Sorcha smiled sweetly. "Yes, that's the one."

Gracie leaned over and whispered in Jen's ear. "Peter Thompson is loaded, owns all kinds of businesses in town. He'd be a catch for any woman."

Frank looked dismayed at the news. "I thought you said you weren't ready to date."

"I wasn't. I told him as much. But now I think maybe I'm being silly. Five years is a long time, after all, and everyone else seems to be moving right along." Frank looked down at his tea and apparently decided that it needed more sugar.

"Too bad you told him no." Lindy looked happy to hear it.

"Yes, well. He did tell me to call him if I change my mind." She smiled. "It is a woman's prerogative to change her mind, after all. Perhaps I'll call him tomorrow."

. . .

On the ride home from the restaurant, Aunt Sorcha was quiet and Jen finally asked the question she'd been wondering. "Are you serious about calling that Peter fellow?"

Aunt Sorcha sounded tired, "Why not? If Frank's ready to date after just a year, what am I waiting for?"

CHAPTER 15

The next morning over coffee, Aunt Sorcha asked Jen what her plans were for the rest of the weekend.

"I was actually thinking that I might see about renting a car and taking a drive out to the country, maybe spend the night and then slowly make my way back tomorrow." It was something she'd been wanting to do.

"Oh, that sounds like fun. No need to rent a car, though. You can take mine."

"Won't you need it? I really don't mind renting one."

"Don't be silly. Save your money. Ian's here if I need to run to the store and Gracie can come get me tonight. A bunch of us are going to the cinema. You're welcome to come too, of course."

"Thank you. That does sound like fun, but I think I want to do a bit of exploring. You really don't mind if I borrow your car? I'll be back early afternoon tomorrow."

"No, I don't mind at all, and take your time. No need to hurry back."

AN HOUR LATER, JEN'S OVERNIGHT BAG WAS PACKED AND SHE was in Aunt Sorcha's car, heading out of town. She drove slowly around the neighborhood first, to get used to driving on the wrong side of the road. After about ten minutes, though, she was surprised that it felt almost normal. She'd consulted the internet and mapped out a route that would take her a few hours out of the city and along the countryside. She planned to visit a few small seaside villages and get a room when she felt tired and ready to settle in for the night.

It was a lovely day, clear and sunny. Traffic was light as it was a Saturday and she spent a relaxing day exploring several small villages. The first few were in the country and she marveled at the rolling green grass, old stone buildings and occasional castles that she passed along the way. She stopped for a late lunch and enjoyed a hot bowl of chicken vegetable soup at a small cafe along Main Street.

She toured a museum and eventually landed in a charming village overlooking the ocean. She found a room at a cute bed and breakfast that was walking distance to the small downtown, and Carolyn, the owner, was a lovely older woman with a snowy white bob and a cheerful smile. Jen loved the sound of her thick Irish lilt.

"A good place for supper? Well, that's easy enough. You'll want to walk down the road about five minutes or so, to Sullivan's Pub. Best fresh fish you'll find anywhere."

Jen's stomach rumbled. It had been hours since lunch and she was ready to sit and enjoy a good meal. She settled into her room, which was small, but pleasant and cozy with a pink flowered quilt on the double bed and large windows overlooking the bay. She checked her hair, washed her hands, and then made her way down the road to the recommended pub. The sun was just starting to set and the wind coming off the water had picked up. She zipped her coat up a bit further to ward off the wind and picked up her step.

She could see the pub straight ahead. There was smoke swirling out of a chimney and the golden glow of candles shimmered in the window. She liked the look of the place already. When she reached the door, she could hear voices and the low hum of music in the background. It was nearly seven and a Saturday night, so she imagined that it was as busy as it was ever likely to be. She opened the door and made her way in. The restaurant was packed, but there were a few open seats at the bar. She settled into the one that was nearest the window and out of the way of the waitresses passing by with trays of food.

She had just taken her coat off when the bartender saw her and came right over. He looked to be in his forties, and had a contagious smile.

"Welcome. What's your pleasure?"

Jen looked around the pub and saw a woman across the bar lift an almost empty glass of wine.

"I'll have a glass of red wine."

"House merlot okay?"

"Sure, unless you have a cabernet?"

"Just merlot, I'm afraid."

"Then merlot it is. Thank you."

He returned a moment later with the wine and a menu.

"In case you're hungry."

Jen's stomach grumbled again.

"I'd get the fish of the day. Not sure what it was, but it was great."

Jen looked up at the voice coming from her left. It belonged to a handsome man with an impish smile and wavy, reddish-brown hair and blue eyes. He looked Irish, but his accent was American, which was intriguing, especially in this area. The only other American accents she'd heard thus far had been in downtown Dublin, usually businessmen getting a quick lunch.

"Are you from the States?" she asked.

"Boston. I'm here on business. Devon Jameson."

Jen smiled. "Jen Graham, from just outside Bozeman, Montana. Devon sounds Irish."

"My grandfather was from here. I still have some family in the area and am staying with them for the weekend before I need to head to the city. What about you?"

"I'm here for a few months, staying with friends and doing

some research. I'm a writer. A romance writer," she added, anticipating the question of what she wrote.

"Impressive. What are you researching, then?"

"Mostly trying to get the feel of the culture right. I've been working out of a friend's software company to learn more about what that's like, as it's the setting for my story."

That seemed to interest Devon. "Which company? I work in the software space, too."

"Roadrunner. Their software speeds up the performance of network applications. I think that's it, anyway."

Devon laughed. "That sounds right to me. I'm familiar with them."

The bartender came by and asked if she was ready to order.

"I heard the fish special was good. I'll have that."

"You'll love it," Devon said.

"So what do you do?" Jen asked.

"I'm in business development. Sales, really. The company I work for is headquartered here but I work out of the Boston and New York offices mostly. Once or twice a year, they fly me in to Dublin."

"Are you here long?"

"No. Just for a week. I fly back home on Friday. I have meetings in Dublin on Wednesday and Thursday. But I'll be there Tuesday night if you feel like hanging out with a fellow American?" He grinned and Jen couldn't help but laugh. He was charming and easy to talk to. It would be fun to have a new friend to go out with. They lived on opposite sides of the country, so she knew she wasn't likely to run into him again after Tuesday.

"Sure, I'd like that. I don't know many people here yet. It's nice to meet a fellow American."

They chatted for another ten minutes or so, until Devon's beer was empty and the bartender brought Jen's dinner over. He put some money down to pay his tab, stood up and held out his hand.

"It was great to meet you, Jen. I'll leave you to enjoy your dinner and I'll be in touch about Tuesday. But plan on it. What's your number?" She gave it to him and then he was on his way. Funny to think that in her quest to explore more of Ireland that she would run into someone from her own country. It made her realize how small the world really was. She took a sip of her wine and nodded when the bartender asked if she'd like another. After finishing dinner, she would head back to the bed and breakfast, climb into her pajamas and read in bed for a bit. All in all, it was turning out to be a perfect day.

CHAPTER 16

Monday morning came much too early. Ian was quieter than usual as they started driving into the city. She'd gotten home mid-afternoon the day before and Ian was out. Aunt Sorcha had explained that he'd met Nadine to drop off Ella and was then heading to Cal's to have dinner and watch some sport that they followed.

"How was the rest of your weekend?" Ian asked as they drove along.

"Fun. It was great to explore a bit." She told him about the villages she visited and the pub she had dinner at.

"You had dinner by yourself at a pub? Did anyone try to pick you up?" he asked casually.

"No, nothing like that. I did meet a really nice guy that happened to be sitting next to me. He was also American, so we started talking."

"And he asked you out?" Ian teased.

"Not really. We might grab a bite to eat when he's in the city, though. He's only in town for a few days."

"Right. He asked you out."

Jen laughed. "It's not like that." Though she realized it probably sounded exactly like that.

"Okay." He grew quiet again and Jen just stared out the window. Ian was hard to read sometimes. He couldn't possibly have a problem with her meeting someone for dinner, could he?

JEN AND MERRY WENT TO MAX'S DELI FOR LUNCH. AS USUAL, there was a wait and almost every table was taken. As soon as one opened up, Jen grabbed it while Merry placed their order. A few minutes later, they were settled and eating their sandwiches.

"You didn't get one for Ian?" Jen asked when she saw that Merry only had two sandwiches on the tray.

"I asked, but he said he was all set. He's been a bit of a grouch today."

"Do you know why?"

"No idea. So tell me all about your weekend. Did you do anything interesting? We did nothing, Absolutely nothing except stay in and watch movies. It was great, though."

Jen filled her in about bingo and her spur of the moment trip and the new friend she made at the pub.

"What did you say his name was?" Merry looked puzzled.

"Devon Jameson."

"I don't know why but that name sounds so familiar. Did he say what company he worked for?"

"No, just that it was some kind of software company. He'd heard of Roadrunner, though."

"Hmmm. Well, anyway, that's exciting that he wants to take you to dinner. Could this be a new romance?"

"No, we live on opposite ends of the country. I don't really think of him that way and I didn't get that sense from him, either. I think it's just that we had fun talking and are both American and he'll be in Dublin, so why not?"

"Right, why not?"

MERRY POPPED INTO JEN'S OFFICE A LITTLE EARLIER THAN

usual for their mid-afternoon coffee break. She came in quietly and Jen was surprised to see her shut the door firmly behind her. She leaned on the edge of Jen's desk and then looked around as if to make sure no one was listening.

"So, your new friend Devon?" She paused for dramatic effect and Jen waited for her to continue.

"He works for Spry Software. That's our main competitor, the one we are going up against for MacMurray's account. He's their VP of Sales. They probably flew him in to help close the deal."

"Oh, really? He definitely didn't mention the name of his company. I would have remembered that."

"Did he ask you any questions about Roadrunner?"

"No. He, just seemed interested that I go in each day to work here."

"Hmm, and then he asked you out to dinner. For Tuesday night? Not Wednesday or Thursday?"

"No, he said he had client meetings on those days."

"Right, one of them is MacMurray. I bet he's going to try to pump you for information before he goes in."

Jen sighed. "I don't think so. He could have done that at the pub, and he didn't."

Merry almost looked disappointed. "Maybe not. I'd still be careful what you say to him. Not that you really know anything worth sharing."

"That's true. Well, I'm ready for a coffee. It's pouring out, though. Should we just grab one in the kitchen?"

"Definitely. I don't have an umbrella."

As they walked into the kitchen, Ian was there, brewing a cup as well. He looked up and smiled when he saw them.

"Afternoon, ladies. You look like you've been deep in conversation."

Jen and Merry exchanged glances. Ian chuckled. "Jen must have told you about her date tomorrow."

Merry's mouth dropped. "You told Ian, too?"

"I didn't think it was a big deal," Jen said uncomfortably.

"What did you say his name was? Dan something?" Ian

asked.

"Devon Jameson."

The room went deathly quiet.

"Where did you say he worked?" he asked.

"I didn't. He didn't mention it."

"He works at Spry. I looked him up," Merry said.

"I see. And are you still going?" His tone was cold.

"I don't know. He hasn't called yet. Do you not want me to go?"

Ian stared at her coldly. "Do whatever you want."

He stormed off with his coffee and Merry shook her head. "I'm sorry about that. He can be a real grouch sometimes."

Jen didn't care much for his behavior. In fact, his attitude quite annoyed her. "What does he think is going to happen? That I'd spill all the company secrets? I don't even know anything!"

"Don't worry about it. Just go and have fun. It will be interesting to see if he tries to get any information out of you."

THE RIDE HOME WAS A QUIET ONE. IAN BARELY SPOKE EXCEPT to the various people that called him. He did seem to notice, though, during a moment of silence when her phone beeped, indicating that she had a new text message. It was from Devon confirming plans to meet up at Christo's Restaurant after work the next day. Jen texted back confirming.

"I take it you're going?" Ian asked a few minutes later, assuming correctly who the message was from.

"Yes, I am. I'm looking forward to a night out with a new friend. It should be fun."

Ian didn't say another word for the rest of the ride home, and told Aunt Sorcha when they walked in that he wasn't hungry and wouldn't be joining them for dinner.

Aunt Sorcha raised her eyebrows, as Ian strode by them and disappeared upstairs. "Well, he's in a mood, isn't he? Looks like it's just the two of us for dinner."

CHAPTER 17

J en took extra care with her outfit the next day, since she was going out straight from work. She wore her favorite black dress pants instead of jeans and a soft, dusty rose sweater with a flattering v-neck. Instead of pulling her hair up in a ponytail like she usually did, she left it down and straight. Ian smiled tightly when he saw her come into the kitchen.

"Ready to go?" he asked.

"I'm ready."

The ride in was a quiet one. Ian seemed preoccupied and not in the mood for conversation. Jen read a book on her iPhone and was glad when the short ride in was over. She went straight to her office and buried herself in her writing for the rest of the day. She ate a salad at her desk for lunch and by the time five o'clock rolled around, she wasn't even in the mood to go out anymore. She just felt like going home and crawling into bed. She hated when there was tension of any kind and she was annoyed at Ian's behavior at the same time.

He was still in his office when she locked her laptop in her office and grabbed her purse to go meet Devon. She didn't want to be lugging the laptop and her notebook and tote bag around all night and knew she wasn't going to need them. Ordinarily, she brought them home with her and always hopped online at some point during the evening to write or edit or just check Facebook.

Devon had said that Christo's restaurant was a short walk from her office. She set out in what she hoped was the right direction and was glad to see the restaurant sign after she'd walked past a few streets. She smelled garlic before she reached the front door and it was an intoxicating scent. When she walked in, Devon was waiting by the front desk, checking email on his phone. He looked up and smiled when he saw her.

"Great to see you." He pulled her in for a friendly hug and then the host, an older Italian gentleman, led them to their table. Jen looked around as they walked and liked what she saw. Flickering candles were on every table, along with crisp, white linen cloths and burgundy napkins. The restaurant was half full which was a good sign for a quiet Tuesday night, she supposed. The host handed them each a menu after they sat down.

"Have you been here before?" Jen asked as someone stopped by their table to fill their water glasses and then returned a moment later with a basket of warm bread.

"Yeah, I come here at least once on every visit. Food's great and it's right around the corner from our office, too."

"Oh, I didn't realize that."

Their waiter came by and Devon ordered a bottle of chianti. Once it was opened and they each had a glass, Devon lifted his and smiled. "Cheers!"

They tapped glasses and placed their order a moment later —ravioli with meat sauce for her and lasagna for him.

"I have a confession to make," Devon began with a mischievous gleam in his eye.

"Oh?" Jen was enjoying herself already. She buttered a piece of bread and popped a bite in her mouth while waiting for him to continue.

"So, there's something I didn't tell you, I don't think, when we met. I work for Spry software." He paused, waiting for a reaction of some sort, but Jen didn't give him one.

"Oh, that's nice. Do you like it there?"

He chuckled. "Yeah, it's a great place to work." He took a sip of wine, then set his glass down. "We're a competitor of Roadrunner. We're actually going up against you guys for a huge account. That's why I'm here."

"I know."

"You do?" He seemed surprised and a bit relieved.

"I didn't make the connection, but my friend Merry, who is Ian's executive assistant, did. She wondered if you might try to pump information out of me."

He laughed. A genuine belly laugh, and Jen smiled. She trusted that her gut instincts about Devon had been right. He wasn't after information.

"No, if that had been what I was after, I would have stuck around the night I met you, bought you a few more drinks and then tried to get you to open up. That's not really my style. Besides, I suspect that you probably don't know anything that could really help us anyway."

"Probably not," Jen agreed.

"Ultimately, it's going to come down to who they like better and who they think will better fit their customer needs." He topped off both of their glasses. "I just thought you were cool and might want to keep a lonely fellow American company over a good Italian meal."

"That's what I thought, too," Jen said.

They chatted easily about everything under the sun and when their meals came, they were excellent.

"Their pasta here is almost as good as my mother's, though I could never tell her that," Devon said.

"I didn't know Irish women were known for good pasta?"

"My dad's side of the family is Irish. My mother's is from Sicily. Her homemade ravioli and sauce are ridiculous."

They were too full for dessert, but each had a coffee with a small glass of licorice flavored Sambuca on the side.

"So, how is Ian to work with? He's a friend of the family?" Devon asked.

"He's the cousin of my best friend in Montana. I'm staying with her aunt and he's there for a few weeks as well while his condo is being renovated. We don't really work together. I'm just using an empty office to work out of and picking as many brains as possible to get a good understanding of what people do in software companies, what it's like to work there."

"You mentioned your story has a setting like that?"

Jen nodded.

"Well, I can give you the perspective from the sales side. It's an extremely competitive business. You could be the market leader one month and then the company chasing you comes out with a better way of doing something, even a tiny enhancement and suddenly you're no longer in first place."

"Does that happen often?"

"All the time. It's a stressful business, to be sure, and competitors try to undercut each other on price to win the business. Everyone does that when they need to."

"That does sound stressful." It sounded horrible to Jen, but by the gleam in Devon's eye she could tell that he enjoyed it.

"It's a game to you, isn't it?"

"What do you mean?" He looked slightly unsure what she was getting at.

"Closing the deal, winning the business. You love it."

He smiled. "I do. It's a rush, for sure. And I'm pretty good at it. We don't win them all, though. I'd say our odds for MacMurray's business are a little worse than 50/50. It's always harder to win the business than it is to keep it."

"That makes sense."

"Ian's a sharp guy, though. I admire him. What he and Cal have done with the company is impressive." He paused for a moment and then a mischievous gleam came into his eyes. "Rumor is he lives and breathes the business, and that he keeps a cot in his office for when he pulls an all-nighter. Is that true?"

"Wow. A cot? I don't think so. I haven't seen one, anyway. He usually leaves at a normal hour. Maybe he used to do that. I don't really know."

"Probably just a rumor. You know how people talk."

"True."

Devon glanced at his cell phone, which was vibrating. He

didn't take the call, but did hand a credit card to the waiter when he came by. Jen offered to chip in but he refused. "Absolutely not. I invited you, and you saved me from a night of boredom in my hotel room. I'm glad you agreed to come out tonight. This was fun."

When they exited the restaurant, Devon flagged a taxi and gave the driver a stack of cash.

"He'll take you wherever you need to go. Jen, it was great seeing you. Maybe our paths will cross again someday."

"Thanks, Devon. I'd wish you good luck tomorrow, but well, you know." Jen grinned as she climbed into the cab.

CHAPTER 18

D id you have a good time last night, dear?" Aunt Sorcha asked over coffee in the kitchen the next day. Jen was up early and had just joined her at the kitchen table to eat a quick breakfast of scrambled eggs and toast.

"I did. It was fun. We went to a lovely restaurant." She told her all about Christo's and went into detail about the food as she knew she would appreciate it.

Aunt Sorcha had a wistful expression as she said, "I haven't been there. I don't get into the city so much anymore, but it sounds wonderful. There's a nice Italian restaurant here too, Gina's. Maybe I'll suggest that to Peter when he calls to confirm for Friday."

"You called him? And set a date to go out? That's exciting." Jen was happy for her.

"I did. Everyone else is dating. I might as well, right?"

"Yes, I think it's a great idea. And he sounds very nice."

"Hmmm. He's nice enough. A bit boring, actually. But maybe I just don't know him well enough yet."

"Just go have fun, and a good dinner!"

"How was your young man? Will you see him again?"

Ian came into the kitchen as Aunt Sorcha asked the question. He stopped, looked at Jen and said nothing.

Jen smiled at Aunt Sorcha. "He was very nice, and charming. It was a fun night. But, no, I don't expect I'll be seeing him again. He heads back to the States on Friday."

"Oh, that's too bad." Aunt Sorcha looked disappointed.

"A pity," Ian agreed cheerfully. "Are you about ready to go?"

IAN SEEMED IN A GOOD MOOD ON THE DRIVE IN. AS THEY DROVE Jen wondered about something Devon had said over dinner.

"Do you have a cot in your office?" she asked.

Ian glanced sideways at her. "What?"

She repeated the question.

He chuckled. "I do, actually."

"Really? I thought that was just a rumor. I didn't remember seeing one there."

"It's in a closet. I haven't used it in over a year, but I used to every now and again when we were just getting going and I worked longer hours. How did you know about it?"

"Devon mentioned it. He asked me if it was true."

Ian frowned. "What else did he ask you?" Jen knew that he was worried that Devon was fishing for information.

"Nothing. He was actually quite complimentary about you, and Cal. Said you're both known for being brilliant, hard workers."

"Oh. Well, that's nice to hear, I suppose. Did he say anything else?"

"He doesn't seem at all sure of their chances. Said your company has the edge."

Ian nodded.

"We do. But it may not be enough."

CHAPTER 19

Ian looked up when he saw Jen walk by his office on her way to the kitchen. Her swinging ponytail had caught his eye and made him smile. She waved as she passed by, and he got up for a minute and walked around his office, stretching his legs. He looked out the large window that spanned the corner of his office and overlooked the city from ten floors up. It was an impressive view, but his mind was stuck on Jen.

Was it because she'd made it clear that a romance between them was off-limits that made him so curious about her? It didn't help that she was just a few rooms away at his mother's house and right down the hall in the office. It would be easier when he moved back into his condo, which should be soon. Eric, the contractor, had left a message on his cell that he anticipated finishing by the end of the week. Maybe then, his life would get back to normal.

His phone flashed. It was Merry, which probably meant she was screening a call for him.

"Hi, Merry."

"Jim MacMurray's calling. Shall I put him through?"

"Yes, thank you."

"Ian?" His voice was so cheerful that Ian wondered what was coming.

"Hi, Mr. MacMurray. I hope you are calling with good news."

"Well, yes, I think you might consider it good news. I'm calling to invite you to dinner at my home Friday night. I'd like you to meet my wife and for us to get to know each other a little better. Oh, and be sure to bring your houseguest, Jen. My wife wants to meet her. Turns out she's read all of her books. Small world, eh?"

Ian was stunned. "Yes, yes it is. What time would you like us there?"

"How about half past six?"

IAN HUNG UP THE PHONE AND TYPED JEN'S NAME INTO GOOGLE. The search results brought up page after page of book links, blog posts and award mentions. He clicked on the top link which brought him to USA Today, where he saw that her most recent release listed in the top one hundred on the USA Today Bestsellers list. The link there took him to Amazon where he could see all of her books and their colorful covers and hundreds of reviews, most of them four and five stars. He'd had no idea she was so successful. He was surprised and proud at the same time. He just hoped she didn't mind joining him for dinner Friday night. It might not be her idea of a good time.

He decided to go down to her office and find out. When he tapped on her door, she looked up in surprise and waved for him to come in.

"I hope I'm not interrupting?"

"Not at all. I was just stirring some sugar into my coffee and thinking about what to write next."

"I looked you up. I didn't realize you had so many books out and recently hit the USA Today list. That's impressive. Was it your first time?"

Was Jen blushing? She hesitated for a moment and then

said, "No, I've hit it before. On my last three books, actually. Still haven't cracked the New York Times list yet, though."

"You will, I have no doubt," he said and meant it.

"Thank you. It's a long-term goal of mine, someday. So, what made you decide to look me up?" Jen raised her eyebrows.

"Jim MacMurray called. He and his wife want us to come to dinner on Friday. Do you mind joining me?"

"Why me?" Jen looked confused.

"Turns out Jim MacMurray's wife is a fan of your books. He hasn't made a decision yet, wants to get to know us better."

"Oh. Well, that's good right?" A mischievous look crossed her face. "I'll go, on one condition?"

"Okay?"

"If you close this deal, you go on vacation, or holiday, as you call it, immediately, for one week. No checking email or calling in for messages."

Ian frowned. He'd planned on taking some time off and now was as good a time as any, but not checking in at all?

"Yes, to going on holiday. But it's not realistic to ask me not to check in."

"I think it is. That's the whole point of a vacation. Unplugging completely. I'm sure Cal would be happy to cover for you and Merry can handle most of the small stuff and forward anything pressing to Cal."

"I suppose that could work."

"All right, then. I'd be delighted to join you for dinner Friday night."

"Great. I owe you one. Thank you."

CHAPTER 20

O n Friday, Jen and Ian left work at five sharp to go home, change quickly and then head out. Jen had hardly seen Ian for the past few days, except for the ride to and from the office. He'd gone straight up to his apartment and back to work. Aunt Sorcha just shook her head and after an hour or so, brought him a tray of whatever they'd had for supper.

"He works too hard. I'd hoped having you here might get him out more, but it's all he does. I don't think it's healthy. He's worse than ever this week."

Jen decided to put her mind at ease a bit. "I think he may be doing extra work now so he can take some time off soon."

Aunt Sorcha had brightened at that news. "Do you really think so? That would be marvelous. I don't remember the last time that boy went on holiday."

"If he closes this big deal with the people we are going to meet for dinner on Friday, then he's going on vacation, effective immediately." She grinned. "I made him promise to unplug totally, no email or phone allowed."

Aunt Sorcha looked stunned. "He agreed to that? That's wonderful."

"He did."

But now it seemed he might be regretting that agreement

and looking for a way he could get out of it, or at least rene-gotiate.

"So, what if I check in once a day, just email?" he asked as they drove to the MacMurray's.

Jen stuck to her guns.

"Absolutely not. A deal's a deal. You'll thank me after. You'll see."

"What am I going to do with myself?" Ian wondered out loud.

Jen laughed. "Relax, of course! Do whatever strikes your fancy that is non-work related. Maybe you could show me around some, play tourist."

Ian considered the idea. "I could do that. There's a few really cool places I could show you, all within a few hours' drive."

"I'm up for anything. I'd like to see as much as possible while I'm here."

"Okay, I'll give that some thought. After all, if I'm on holi-day, you will be, too. At least from working in the office."

"That's fine with me. I was hoping to do some exploring while I was here."

"We'll make sure to do that, then."

The MacMurrays lived about an hour north of Aunt Sorcha's house. After a while, Ian pulled onto a lovely, wooded street with large homes on beautifully manicured lawns.

"That's it, I think. Number 22." Ian pulled into the driveway of an elegant older home. There was a circular driveway in front. He parked there and Jen grabbed the bag with the bottle of wine they'd picked up along the way. They walked to the front door and before they could ring the bell, the door opened and Jim MacMurray was standing there.

"I heard your car come up the drive. Nice to see you again, Jennifer."

"You too, Mr. MacMurray. We brought some wine." She handed him the bottle.

"Thank you, and please call me Jim. I'll give this to Caro-line. She'll know what to do with it. Follow me."

He led them down the hall to the kitchen, where a white-haired woman in a pale blue sweater, was tossing a salad in a large wooden bowl. She looked up and smiled when they walked in.

"Caroline, I'd like you to meet Ian and Jennifer. They brought some wine."

"Oh, how thoughtful. So nice to meet you both. Why don't I open this and let it breathe a bit before dinner? I have another bottle open if you'd like to enjoy a glass now?"

They both nodded and she set off to pour the wine. A moment later, she handed them each a glass.

"Why don't we go into the other room and get comfortable? The roast has another twenty minutes or so to go." She led them into a beautiful living room, with plush white sofas that sank way down when you sat on them. The view to the backyard was spectacular. There were twinkling lights lining a back patio and a lush garden just beyond.

"Have you lived here very long?" Jen asked as she held tightly to her wine glass, careful not to tip and spill the red wine onto the very white sofa.

"Thirty years as of last month," Jim said proudly. "We raised two children here. They're both married and one of them has kids of their own now."

"We're lucky that they still live nearby. I get to see my grandchildren often. Every Tuesday, at a minimum. That's my day with them, and it gives their mother a break."

"I'm sure she must love that," Jen said.

Caroline leaned forward. "I hope you don't mind that I asked Jim to invite you to come along with Ian this evening. I was just so excited when he told me that he'd met you and that you were staying in the area for a bit. I've read all your books and just loved them."

"Thank you so much. I was happy to come. Thank you for inviting me."

"So, Ian, what do you like to do in your spare time?" Jim asked as he sipped his drink. Jen wasn't sure what it was, something dark on ice.

Ian chuckled. "I don't have a whole lot of spare time. But I suppose most of my free time, when I'm not working, is spent with my daughter, Ella. She's six."

"She's adorable," Jen added with a smile.

Jim glanced at Jen then back at Ian. "That's wonderful that you get to spend time with your daughter. Family is so important. A man needs a hobby, though. Some kind of interest outside of work. If you weren't so busy, what might interest you?"

Ian thought about that. "I haven't played in a long time, but I do enjoy golf."

"Well, there you go then! Start playing again. It's great exercise. I try to get in at least a game every other week or so, sooner if I can manage it. Caroline plays, too."

"Do you golf, Jen?" Caroline asked.

"No, I never have. Is it very hard to learn? My parents always loved to play. My mother is in a ladies' league."

"I'm in one here, too. Every Thursday. We have a great time. The club I go to gives lessons on the weekends. If you have time while you're here, that might be fun for you."

That did sound fun. She doubted she would have time while she was in Ireland, but it was something she'd thought about trying. Maybe she'd look into lessons next spring.

Caroline stood up. "If you'll excuse me, I'm going to go take the roast out of the oven."

"Can I help you with anything?" Jen offered.

"No, thank you, dear. Why don't you all make your way into the dining room and get settled. I'll be there in a few minutes."

They followed Jim into the dining room and to a large round table that was set for four. Jen sat next to Ian and Jim was on the other side of him. The roast smelled amazing as Caroline carried it into the room on a large platter. It was surrounded by roasted potatoes and glazed carrots. A basket of what looked like muffins sat next to a dish of softened butter.

"Jim if you could do the slicing honors?" Caroline asked. She went back to the kitchen and returned a moment later with a wineglass and the bottle that they'd brought. She poured herself some and when Jen and Ian finished the last sips left in their glasses, she refilled them with the new wine.

"This is delicious," she said as she took a sip. Jen had to agree. It was rich and smooth and she knew it would go wonderfully with the roast beef. Jim cut a bunch of slices and they all helped themselves to everything. Once their plates were full and they were about to dive in, Jim raised his glass in a toast.

"To new friends and valued partnerships!"

Jen glanced at Ian. That sounded promising. Ian caught her eye and smiled. He then directed his gaze toward his host and then his wife as he clinked his glass against theirs.

"And to a dinner that looks amazing. Thank you," he said.

Caroline looked pleased. "It was my pleasure. That's Yorkshire pudding, it's always served with roast beef here," she explained when she saw Jen hesitate as she reached for one.

The Yorkshire Pudding was light and fluffy and delicious with the butter. They chatted easily as they ate and the conversation shifted from the MacMurray's recent trip to the East Coast of the US.

"We've been all up and down the East Coast, but haven't been out West yet. I hear it's beautiful where you live, in Montana?" Caroline said.

"It is. I do love it there. But I've never lived anywhere else. I think it's beautiful here, too."

"It's home for us," Jim said. "I think I could happily live in a lot of the places I've visited, though. Caroline is more the homebody. I don't think she'd agree to move."

Caroline chuckled. "He's right about that. I've lived here all my life and can't imagine being anywhere else. Though it always is fun to explore other places. I couldn't leave my kids, though."

"I imagine I'll be here for many more years to come, because of Ella, but also now that my father is gone, I like to be near my mother, too."

"How long has it been for your mother?" Caroline asked.

"About five years now."

"She's probably about my age, I'd guess?"

Ian nodded.

"Is she dating at all? A dear family friend might be a possibility for her. He lost his wife about a year ago and I've heard that he's just started to date."

"I don't know about that," Ian said.

"She might be," Jen said. "I know she was just recently talking about going out with someone."

Ian looked surprised. "My mother said that?"

Jen laughed. "Yes, she did."

"Well, check with her. If she's interested, I'll tell Frank to call her." Caroline said.

"Frank? What's his last name?" It couldn't be the same person, could it?

"Whitman. He's a dear man."

Ian caught Jen's eye and they both laughed.

"It truly is a small world. They already know each other. Frank lives right around the corner from my mother," Ian said.

"You don't say? How interesting. Well, I guess we'll just let things happen on their own, then, if they are meant to do so."

Jen helped Caroline to clear the plates when they finished and carried a tray of brownies in for dessert. Caroline made coffee and even though she was stuffed, Jen couldn't resist having a brownie. Ian and Jim both had two.

"Once you're back golfing again, you let me know," Jim said at the end of the evening. He held front door open and they said their goodbyes.

"Oh, and by the way, I might as well let you know now, since I've made my decision. We'll be doing a deal together, if you're still interested.

Ian beamed. "Of course we are. Thank you. You won't regret it."

"I'd better not!"

Jen waved as they drove away and as soon as they were out of the driveway, Ian turned to her, "Thank you so much for coming. I don't think that could have gone any better."

"Congratulations! On closing the deal…and starting your vacation."

"Thanks." He was quiet for a few minutes and then said, "About that…"

"Don't even think about it. A deal's a deal. You're going off the grid. Effective immediately."

Ian chuckled. "You drive a hard bargain. Okay, then…" He was still grinning as they drove along. Rain started to fall, softly at first, then it quickly turned to a torrential downpour. He slowed as they came around a corner and then they both noticed a loud thumping sound. There was a gas station down the road and Ian pulled in. He jumped out in the pouring rain and walked over to Jen's side and took a close look at the rear tire. A few minutes later, he was back in the car, soaked from head to toe.

"Is it flat?" Jen asked.

"Totally. I must have punctured it on the way over." He sat quietly for a few minutes as the rain came down even harder. Then he pulled out his phone and pulled up the internet. His fingers flew furiously, typing away. Finally, he looked up.

"Weather forecast has it being like this for several hours. It's late now, almost ten. There's a hotel right up the road. I noticed it earlier. We could stay there for the night, then get this taken care of in the morning. I just don't dare risk driving further and I don't know about you but I don't really want to sit here in the rain for hours waiting for roadside service to come."

"That's fine."

Ian drove slowly up the street to a small hotel. He parked and they went into the lobby where an older woman was working the front desk. She smiled when she saw them.

"Do you have any available rooms for the night?" he asked.

"You're in luck. I have one. It's our last available."

"Great, we'll take it." Ian handed her his credit card and a few minutes later she returned it along with the room key. "You're on the third floor, at the end of the hall."

They made their way to the room and Jen held her breath

as Ian opened the door. She was hoping there were two double beds, but knew that was more of an American thing. Sure enough, the room was lovely and spacious, but there was just one bed.

"I'm sorry. I know this is a bit awkward," Ian said and then added, "I promise to stay on my side."

"You'd better," Jen teased, and then added, "I know it's not your fault." She started to walk toward the bathroom and tripped over the rug. Ian grabbed her so she wouldn't fall and she awkwardly straightened up. He still held onto her, though, longer than necessary. The vibe in the air changed, became charged and Ian smiled.

"I don't suppose you'd want to take advantage of the situation we find ourselves in?" He ran a finger lightly down her arm and she shivered. It was so tempting to just give in and see where things went. She wanted nothing more than for him to kiss her, but she knew if she encouraged that and what would likely follow, that she would have regrets in the morning. Still, it was hard for her to voice the words, to actually say no, so she stayed silent a moment longer, not wanting the closeness to end.

Ian took her hesitation for a refusal, let go of her arms and stepped back.

"Well, you can't blame me for asking." He walked over to the window while Jen went into the bathroom, washed her face and hands and then left the door open for Ian to use it. She slipped into the bed and gathered the covers around her. It was a double bed, so there was plenty of room for both of them.

A few minutes later, Ian came over to the bed and climbed in next to her. It was still raining hard outside and the rhythmic pounding against the windows was somehow soothing. Jen found herself relaxing as she listening to the steady sound of it.

"Are you sleepy?" Ian asked softly.

"Not yet, but I think I will be soon. It's getting late, and I'm full from a great dinner and wine. It was a good night."

"It was. They're nice people."

"They seem really happy, and have been married for a long time."

"My parents were like that, too. I think that's why it's been hard for my mother to move on."

"She seems almost ready. What was he like, your father?"

"He was incredibly smart, a successful businessman. My happiest memories of him were playing ball as a kid. Course that didn't happen often, as he was always working."

"That sounds familiar," Jen said. It explained a lot.

Ian chuckled. "I never thought about that, but I suppose you're right. He was always working. Nights, weekends. He was home, but he wasn't really there, his mind and attention was elsewhere."

"Do you think he ever regretted that?"

Ian was quiet for a moment. "Maybe. He slowed down at the end, when he retired, and then threw himself into not working. He and my mother took holiday after holiday. He started golfing more. He always liked to keep busy."

"It sounds like he had a lot of energy."

"That's an understatement. He was so proud when I started the company. I still miss being able to call him whenever something good happened. Now I just call my mother. Which is great too, of course."

"I know what you mean."

Jen felt her eyes grown heavy and turned on her side so her back was toward Ian. She snuggled into her pillow and just as she was drifting off to sleep, she felt an arm wrap around her waist. She tensed up at first then when the arm didn't move, and when she heard a light snoring, she realized that Ian was already asleep. She relaxed and fell fast asleep herself.

CHAPTER 21

Jen woke to sunshine streaming through the hotel window. She was disoriented at first, then quickly remembered the rainstorm and flat tire. She stretched and glanced to Ian's side of the bed and was surprised to see that it was empty. The bathroom door was wide open so he wasn't in there, either. Maybe he went for coffee. She decided to get in the shower and twenty minutes later, she was done and dressed.

There was still no sign of Ian, so she proceeded to comb out her hair and blow it dry. Just as she was finishing up, the hotel door opened and Ian stepped inside. Jen put the hair dryer away and walked out of the bathroom. He was holding two coffees.

"I'm not sure how you take it, so there's cream and sugar on the side."

"Oh, thank you. I wondered if that's where you went."

"I was waiting for the car service to come. They fixed the tire enough that we can get home on it, and then I'll take it in for a replacement."

The sun was shining brightly as they drove home. Ian went a bit slower than usual, just to be on the safe side, and Aunt Sorcha came walking out when they pulled into the driveway.

She met them as they got out of the car.

"Oh, I'm so glad you made it home okay. I've been worried ever since I got your text last night."

"It's fine, just a small puncture. They patched it up, and I'm actually going to run it over to the tire place now to see if I can get it taken care of." He turned to Jen. "Thanks again for coming last night. I really didn't expect that he would let us know his decision right away."

"It was a fun night. I'm happy for you and Cal." She turned to Aunt Sorcha and said, "Ian has some good news to share. He's officially on holiday for the next week!"

Ian frowned. "Right. Well, the good news is we closed our big deal, though Jen here drove a hard bargain. She agreed to accompany me only if I agreed to go on holiday, effective immediately, if we were chosen."

Aunt Sorcha gave her a big hug, and then pulled Ian in for one as well. "Well, of course I'm thrilled you got your deal, but I'm even more excited that you agreed to slow down a little and take a proper holiday. Sometimes you remind me of your father a bit too much. Jen, I can't thank you enough for this."

Jen smiled. "I was happy to help. And selfishly I'm hoping Ian might do some sightseeing with me. There's still so much I want to see while I'm here."

"That sounds like a good plan. Oh, and you're both going to come to the barbecue tonight I hope? Frank and Gracie and all the neighbors will be there. I'm sure I mentioned it to you earlier this week?"

Yes, she had mentioned it repeatedly, and Frank's name more than once. Jen was looking forward to it.

"You said it's like a pot luck. Everyone brings something, right?"

"Yes, you can make whatever you like, dear. Maybe something fun that you have often in Montana?"

Jen thought about that. She liked to cook, especially when she had people over for dinner or a party. Maybe she would make one of her favorite appetizer recipes. Her taco bean dip was always a hit.

"I have something in mind. I'll need to run to the store, though, for the ingredients."

"I need to get a few last minute things, too. We can run out together."

"All right, then. I'll see you ladies later." Ian went off to get his car fixed while Jen followed Aunt Sorcha into the kitchen so they could make a list of what they needed.

"SOMETHING SMELLS GOOD," IAN SAID AS HE WALKED INTO THE kitchen a few hours later.

"Thanks. It's a taco dip." Jen opened a can of pinto beans and mashed them up in a hot pan with a bit of oil until they were like the refried beans she had at home. She stirred them into the browned and seasoned ground beef along with a handful of shredded cheddar cheese and mixed until the cheese was melted and everything was well blended.

"Need a taste tester?"

"Sure." She took a tortilla chip and scooped a generous amount of dip on to it and handed it to him.

"Oh, that's really good."

"What are you making?" she teased him. Ian was rarely in the kitchen.

"My specialty. Garlic Honey Chicken Wings."

"Really?"

Ian chuckled. "Yep. I just placed the order, and now I have to go pick them up. Be back soon."

Jen was still smiling when Aunt Sorcha wandered in and tried a taste of the dip, too.

"Oh, that's lovely. I'm going to want the recipe."

She went to the refrigerator and took out two lemon meringue pies and set them on the counter.

"Frank's making burgers and his famous pulled pork and Gracie, of course, is bringing fruit scones. I think we'll have plenty of food. I'm going to just walk these over to Frank's house and see if he needs a hand with anything. I'll be back to get you shortly and then we can head over. Ian will know to go straight there."

Aunt Sorcha popped her pies in a box and then left to deliver them. Jen turned the heat to warm. It was nice to have the house to herself for a bit. She'd been relieved earlier, that there had been no awkwardness between her and Ian. If she'd given in to her physical attraction to him, there might well have been, so she was glad that she had resisted. It had been so tempting, though.

The more time she spent around Ian, the more she liked him. And learning about his father and his workaholic ways helped to understand why he was so driven. It was what he'd grown up seeing. She was glad, and a bit surprised, that he'd agreed to take the time off. She hoped that he really would spend some of it playing tourist with her. Her story was going well, but it always helped her to go deeper when she could experience a place first hand and immerse herself in it.

Jen was lost in her thoughts when she heard footsteps walking through the door. She was surprised to see that it was Ian instead of Aunt Sorcha. He smiled when he saw her.

"I just dropped off the wings and Mam asked if I wouldn't mind coming back to get you. She was deep in conversation with Frank and said she needed to show him how to do something in the kitchen."

Jen chuckled. "That sounds about right. Let me just pour this into a casserole dish and we can go.

Ten minutes later, they arrived at Frank's and Jen set her warm dish of dip on a long folding table that was set up outside. She poured the tortilla chips into a large bowl and set those down, too, right next to Ian's platter of wings.

I should have kissed her last night. The thought had crossed Ian's mind more than once as he and Jen made their way over to where his mother and Frank were putting out a tray of pulled pork. It had been so hard to not just pull her towards him and crush his lips against hers. He could sense that she would have allowed it, but she'd stayed silent and that spoke volumes to him. When they finally kissed, and he was determined that would happen, it would be when Jen made it clear that she had no hesitation, that she wanted it as much as he did.

"Try a taste of Frank's pulled pork. It's the best I've ever had." His mother handed him a plastic fork with a bite of perfectly charred meat. He gave a thumbs up as he chewed and couldn't help noticing that his mother was beaming as she stood next to Frank. Her smile grew tight, though, as a newer neighbor made her way over to the table and gave a big hug to both Frank and his mother, who was glaring the whole time.

The newcomer's hair was big and blonde and her makeup was heavy. She was wearing too much perfume and was loaded up with all kinds of jewelry—gold bracelets, diamond earrings and the biggest diamond ring he'd ever seen. He took a step back when she turned and focused her attention on him.

"Oh, this must be your son. Ed, is it? I'm Lindy." She held out her hand and then nodded at Jen. "Nice to see you again."

"It's Ian," he corrected her.

"Oh, right, sorry." She turned her attention back to Frank and made a big production out of setting down her casserole dish next to Frank's tray meat, and shoving his mother's lemon pies out of the way.

"Makes sense this should be right here, don't you think?" she said in a sugary sweet voice. "Frankie, this is the cole slaw I told you about. My mother's secret recipe. It should be just fabulous with your amazing pork."

"Oh, that sounds good." Frank looked uncomfortable being the center of attention.

Jen caught Ian's eye and looked as though she was trying not to laugh. He vaguely remembered hearing that there was a new woman that rubbed people the wrong way. Now that he'd met her, he could see why. She clearly had set her sights on Frank and that wasn't sitting well with his mother.

"Okay, all the food is out. Everyone help themselves," Frank announced.

They grabbed paper plates and took a bit of everything. There were plastic chairs set up on the lawn and everyone was chatting and eating. Ian went back for more of Jen's dip, which was a big hit. After everyone finished eating and most of the food except for the desserts had been cleared away, the entertainment started. Four brothers in their twenties that lived a few doors down set up in Frank's front yard and played a wide range of music for several hours. It was a beautiful night, warm for the time of year, and people danced and enjoyed some wine and beer.

He and Jen mostly sat watching the crowds. He had a few beers and Jen had some red wine. His mother even had a glass of wine and then spent the next hour dancing up a storm with Frank, much to Lindy's dismay. She tried to get his attention but finally gave up when it was obvious that he only had eyes for Ian's mother. The band started to play a slow tune that Ian particularly liked.

"Feel like taking a spin?"

Jen looked surprised, then smiled and stood up. "Sure, why not?"

He led her out to the dance floor, then pulled her toward him and they swayed together to the music. He breathed in the fresh scent of her hair, enjoying the closeness. Jen sighed and moved a little closer and he tightened his hold on her. The song was over too soon. But then they moved right into another slow song as the crowd of dancers had grown. As the song wound down, Jen tried to stifle a yawn and failed.

"Sorry about that. I don't know why I'm so tired," she apologized.

Ian glanced at his watch. It was half-past ten.

"It's getting late and you're probably still tired from last night. I know I didn't sleep well."

"You're probably right."

"Let's head back. I'll see if my mother wants to join us or stay longer."

They strolled over to where his mother and Frank were sitting side by side in matching lawn chairs, talking softly and laughing. She looked up when they reached them.

"We're going to head back. Are you going to stay for a while?" His mother did not look ready to leave and both of them looked wide awake.

"Yes, we're having too much fun catching up. I'll see you in the morning."

They gathered up the empty casserole dishes and brought them back to the house. Jen quickly loaded them into the dishwasher and then yawned again. Ian smiled and pulled her toward him.

"Sleepy head. Do you mind if I do something that I really wanted to do last night?"

"What?" she asked and then he leaned toward her and her eyes grew big. "Oh!"

He stopped and then looked her intently in the eye. "My feelings for you are not casual. I've been rethinking things quite a bit since I've met you. So, is that a no? Or go?"

This time she didn't hesitate. "Go." He brought his lips down to hers, softly at first, just barely brushing against hers, then he deepened the kiss and she sank into him. After he'd kissed her long and hard, he pulled back and noticed that her cheeks were flushed and her eyes were shining. She'd liked it. Good.

"So, that is a nice way to end an evening. I'll check in with you in the morning, and we can make a plan for where we want to explore first. Sound good?"

"Yes, sounds perfect."

CHAPTER 22

Jen watched him climb the stairs to his apartment and then made her way to her own room, and a few minutes later, climbed into bed. She didn't fall asleep right away, though. Her mind was whirling, switching from replaying that kiss to wondering if it had been a mistake or the start of something important. It didn't feel like a mistake. She couldn't put her finger on what it was, but her feelings about Ian were complicated. He made her nervous and for many reasons, she knew shouldn't let things go any further. If they were to get serious, there would be hurdles to face. Although he'd agreed to the vacation, he was still very much a workaholic. Could he find a balance that she could live with? He also lived in another country. That was a big issue.

He was tied to Ireland because of both his business and his daughter. Her work was portable, so if it came time to compromise in that regard, it would be a bigger change for her. But then the voice of reason took over and reminded her that it was impossible to know how things would unfold this early on in any relationship. All she did know was that she loved being around Ian, spending time with him and his family, and yes, kissing him. Ian had indicated that he might be open to more than a casual fling. She might as well enjoy the rest of her time here, and see where it went.

JEN WOKE EARLY THE NEXT DAY AND WAS THE FIRST ONE UP. SHE made herself a cup of coffee and brought the paper in from the front steps. The house was calm and quiet, and she relaxed in solitude for about an hour, reading the paper and enjoying a second cup of coffee. She had just sat down with her breakfast when Aunt Sorcha wandered in. She'd slept much later than usual.

"Morning, dear," she said as she went to heat a kettle of water for her tea.

"That was a fun party last night. Your neighbors are all very nice," Jen said.

"They are, aren't they," she agreed and then scowled. "Well, except for Lindy. That woman is so annoying."

Jen chuckled. "Frank's pulled pork was amazing."

Aunt Sorcha smiled. "He's a wonderful cook and loves good food. We're going out to a new restaurant in town tonight that we've both been wanting to try." The way she said it almost sounded like they'd been dating for years.

"Oh, how exciting. Your first date!"

"It's just dinner with Frank, a dear old friend," Aunt Sorcha protested.

"Sorry, my mistake. Well, have fun. That sounds marvelous."

"What do you have planned for the rest of the weekend?" The tea kettle whistled, and Aunt Sorcha poured the hot water into her cup and then joined Jen at the kitchen table.

"I'm not sure. Ian mentioned maybe taking a drive somewhere, to see more of the countryside."

"It's a beautiful day for that."

"Absolutely gorgeous," Ian agreed as he came down the stairs and caught Jen's eye. She felt a surge of electricity as their eyes met.

"Morning, dear. I hear you're off on an adventure today," Aunt Sorcha said.

Ian smiled. "We are. I'm not exactly sure where we're going, but it's going to be fun to explore."

CHAPTER 23

Ian and Jen set off an hour later in the BMW. He drove to a small village that Jen had thought looked intriguing but she hadn't stopped in yet. It was quaint and they spent about an hour and a half wandering along Main Street. There were lots of cute little shops, though some of them were closed since it was a Sunday. They got sandwiches to go from one of the stores, and strolled to a pretty park and sat on one of the wrought iron benches to eat. After that, they wandered a bit more then continued on to another town, this one along the ocean.

The rocky beaches were gorgeous and Jen took lots of pictures with her cell phone. She would add the best images to her private Pinterest board that she created for every book. It helped to see the story, to visualize the setting and provided great inspiration. She added to it often and sometimes just looking at the board helped her whenever she was feeling stuck about what needed to happen next.

The air grew cooler as the afternoon passed. There were several museums in this town and by the time they walked about both of them, it was past five and Jen was hungry again. Ian's stomach rumbled and he laughed.

"I don't know about you, but I'm starving already. All this walking around has worked up an appetite. Do you want to duck into a pub and have some dinner? Unless it's too early for you?"

"It's not too early!"

There was a pub a few doors down and they decided to check it out. It was still early so it wasn't too crowded and they were seated right away. Everything sounded good. Jen ordered the steak pie and a glass of red wine and Ian got the shepherd's pie and a draft beer. Their waitress returned right away with their drinks and Ian raised his glass.

"To a wonderful day. I've enjoyed playing tourist with you." Jen loved the small laugh lines around his eyes when he smiled big.

"Thank you for showing me around. I really appreciate it."

"It's been a long time since I've shown someone around like this. I forgot how fun it can be to see places you know and love as if it's the first time."

"What else do you have planned for your week off?"

"Absolutely nothing. It's kind of nice, actually. I might do some reading. I love a good mystery and there's a few books I've been wanting to read, but haven't gotten around to it. And I'd be up for some more day trips. We could even spend some time in Dublin and really explore the city. There's a lot to see there."

"I'd love that. I'm up for anything."

"Good, I'll come up with some plans."

When the waitress brought their food, it smelled and tasted wonderful. As they ate and talked easily about all kinds of things, Jen couldn't help thinking that it was almost going too well. Was this just part of Ian's charm? Or was he serious about being open to more than a fling? When there was a pause in the conversation, she decided to find out more about his dating history.

"Have you dated anyone seriously since your divorce?" she asked.

Ian paused for a moment before answering.

"Yes, twice, in the first year. Both relationships ended badly. The company was firing on all cylinders. We were gearing up to go public and some crazy numbers about my potential net worth were being published." His eyes narrowed and he took a sip of beer before continuing.

"I fell hard for both women, Diane and then Stacy. I thought they were genuinely interested in me. Turns out it was my money. I began to sense it and both times didn't want to believe it. But I overheard Stacey talking about 'landing me' to her mother, and how things would change once we got married."

"What did she mean by that?" Jen was horrified.

"I have no idea but I wasn't about to find out. Diane had a similar conversation with Cal's girlfriend. Not very smart of her. She immediately told Cal, who told me. After that I licked my wounds for a while, and didn't date at all for about six months. That's when I decided that casual relationships where everyone knew what was going on, were the best thing, for me."

"But you feel differently about me?" Jen asked nervously. She needed to be sure that he really was open to more than just a fling.

"I know that you're not interested in anything casual and I respect you for being up front about that with me. It took me a while to get here, but I am open to seeing where things go. I like spending time with you."

He reached out and took her hand, and rubbed his thumb lightly across her palm. Jen shivered from his touch and smiled. "Me, too."

"Good. Did you save room for dessert? I just saw a piece of chocolate cake go by that has my name on it."

Jen laughed. "I'm pretty full, but if you don't mind sharing, I'll have a bite or two of yours and a coffee."

After enjoying the cake and coffee, Ian paid the bill and they made their way back to the car. The temperature had dropped quite a bit and Jen pulled her jacket in tight around her to ward off the wind as they walked. When they reached the car she was about to get in, but Ian came around to her side of the car and pulled her in for a long, slow kiss that made her head spin. He finally came up for air and she shivered as a cold blast of wind whipped through her hair.

"We should probably head back," Ian said and then kissed her again.

———

IT WAS DARK WHEN THEY THEY GOT HOME. AUNT SORCHA WAS watching TV in the living room. She wore a gorgeous sweater that Jen hadn't seen before. It was a pretty blue that made her eyes look even bluer. Jen guessed that she'd only recently gotten home from dinner with Frank.

"How was the new restaurant?" Jen asked.

"It was fantastic! I just got back a few minutes ago. How was your day?"

They told her all about the towns they'd visited and dinner at the pub.

"It's been so long since I've been to either of those places," she said.

"It was more fun than I expected, playing tourist," Ian said with a grin.

Aunt Sorcha looked thoughtful. "I wonder if Frank might want to take a drive to the seaside one of these days?"

"You should do it," Ian said. He yawned and then stood up. "Ladies, if you'll excuse me. I'm going to head to bed. I'll see you in the morning."

"Good night. Thanks for a great day," Jen said happily.

"Good night, dear." Aunt Sorcha watched Ian walk off and then brought her gaze back to Jen.

She had a hard-to-read expression.

"He's a good boy, my Ian. He works too hard, though. You've been a good influence on him."

She looked as though she was going to say something else, but then changed her mind.

"He's a good tour guide," Jen said lightly. "I'm going to head to bed as well. See you in the morning."

She wanted to be respectful of Aunt Sorcha since both she

and Ian were living in her house at the moment. And although things were going well so far, until she was certain that the relationship was solid, she didn't want to be so obvious about it. It would be easier, possibly, when Ian moved back into his condo, which was going to be soon.

She and Ian had talked about that over dinner as well. After his week off, Jen would go into work with him for the next week and by then she would have had a chance to chat with just about anyone in the company who was available to talk to her. Ian would move back after that and Jen would go back to working from home. It seemed like a good plan. She was looking forward to seeing what the rest of the week would bring.

CHAPTER 24

Halfway through the week, Aunt Sorcha figured out that something was going on. Jen and Ian thought they were being so cool around her and that she hadn't the slightest clue that a romance had developed. She let Jen know otherwise that Thursday morning over breakfast.

"So, you and Ian," she said simply.

Jen put down her coffee cup and stared blankly at her. She'd caught her totally off guard.

"What about me and Ian?" she asked cautiously.

"I'm not blind, my dear. I can see that something is brewing between the two of you. I don't have a problem with it. I'm quite fond of you both." She smiled then and Jen relaxed slightly. "But I would urge that you proceed with caution. Take your time and really get to know each other. He's been badly hurt, you know, and doesn't trust easily."

"I know," Jen said quietly.

"Good. So where are you off to today, then? I can hardly keep up with the pair of you this week."

"I think we're going into downtown Dublin. Ian wants to show me his condo and check on the progress of the renovation."

"Oh, marvelous. It's a beautiful condo, but in my opinion it needs a woman's touch. You'll see."

136 PAMELA M. KELLEY

AFTER A MORNING OF TOURING THE CITY AND LUNCH AT ONE OF Ian's favorite neighborhood restaurants, he took her to see his condo. The building was impressive, at least thirty floors high. The concierge at the front desk in the lobby recognized Ian as they approached the elevators.

"Nice to see you. Won't be long before you're moved back in?"

"We're shooting for about a week," Ian confirmed. They went into the elevator and he punched in the top floor.

"You have a penthouse?" Jen asked. That surprised her. Aunt Sorcha's house was modest and aside from the BMW, Ian wasn't at all flashy.

He grinned. "Wait until you see it. They were selling pre-construction when our company went public and it was too good of a deal to pass up."

A few minutes later, the elevator came to a stop and the doors opened. There were only two units on the floor.

"Cal has the other one. We bought them at the same time."

Ian had a penthouse apartment with his best friend as a neighbor. It was surreal.

When Ian opened the door and they walked inside, her jaw dropped. She'd never seen anything quite like his condo. It was huge and the walls were all glass, from floor to ceiling, and wrapped around the whole building. The views were spectacular. The living room had plush, black leather sofas, a glass and metal coffee table and a huge big screen TV. The kitchen had a similar sleek look with black and gray streaked granite countertops, stainless steel appliances and a huge center island with bar- style black chairs along one side. The dining area was still being renovated and waiting for the new flooring to be put down.

"The floor will be the same there. It's a dark cherry hard wood." Around the corner was a large den and game room that was also waiting for new floors. A pool table was in pieces against one wall. Built-in bookcases lined two walls and a gas fireplace was in the corner. Several leather club chairs were in the corners. Once the floors were done, Jen could see that it would be a cozy room.

"I bet you spend a good bit of time in here," Jen said.

"I do. I don't use the pool table as much as I thought I would, but it's still nice to have the option and when I have people over we always seem to gravitate to this room."

He led her down the hall to the bedrooms.

"There's three bedrooms, but I use one as an office. The other is Ella's and then mine of course." The office was the smallest bedroom, but it was still roomy for an office and had gorgeous city views.

"I don't know how you could concentrate with that view."

Ian chuckled. "Well, I'm not usually using it during the day. At night, it's dark."

Ella's room was next and it was exactly as a little girl's room should be, all pinks and creams and a pretty canopy bed in the center of the room.

"That's actually a trundle bed, so if she ever wants to have a friend sleep over, we can just pull out a bed for her."

Ian's was the master bedroom and it was magnificent. The walls were a stormy gray with a hint of blue and the king-size bed was covered with a lighter shade on the blankets and comforter. It was a large room, but it had a warmth to it with the soft colors and, of course, the view was spectacular. A connecting bathroom made Jen gasp as she saw a gorgeous, all-glass shower with tiles in various shades of blue and green. The overall feel was very ocean-like. There was also a jacuzzi tub in the corner and a long marble counter with twin sinks.

"Oh, and there's a lot of closets," Ian said playfully as they walked out of the bathroom and he showed her an enormous walk-in closet that was more than big enough for two people. It even had an island in the center with shelves for shoes.

"I have serious closet envy," Jen said with admiration.

Ian laughed. "I hardly noticed that when I looked at the place. Closets weren't really on my radar. It's a cool place, though, and the location can't be beat. It's less than a ten-minute walk to the office."

"It's perfect for you," Jen agreed.

"I have to admit, I've been happy here. Though it is going to feel quiet after living with you and Mam for these past few weeks."

"Well, I might come visit, if you invite me."

"You're invited." He took her hands and pulled her against him, and they fell onto the bed, laughing and kissing. Just as they were starting to lose themselves in the moment, Ian's phone rang. He ignored it, but then whoever it was called back.

"You should check and see who it is, in case it's something important," Jen said.

Ian sat up and pulled his phone out of his pocket and frowned when he saw the caller ID.

"Hi, Nadine. Is everything okay? How's Ella?" He was quiet for a moment, listening, and then said, "Sure, no problem. I took some time off this week, so I can meet you anytime on Friday if you need to bring her over earlier. Right, okay. I'll talk to you then." He hung up and then turned to Jen. "Ella's coming a little earlier than usual this weekend."

Jen smiled. "I'm sure she'll be excited about that."

"I hope so. Maybe you can spend some time with both of us, too. I was thinking we might take her to the park Saturday afternoon."

"Maybe we can have a picnic? If it's warm enough," Jen suggested.

"That's a great idea. I bet she'd love that."

Jen checked the time and realized it was getting late.

"We should probably head back," she said. "We told your mom we'd be home for dinner. I think she mentioned that Frank is joining us."

"Oh, right. Yes, we should probably go." Ian shut off the lights as they made their way out, and Jen took one last look at the view before they stepped out and into the elevator. She was glad they'd been interrupted by the call from Ian's ex-wife. It would be easy to get caught up in the moment and she agreed with Aunt Sorcha's advice to take things slow. As much as she was enjoying spending time with Ian, they still had the location hurdle and it was a big one. If they kept things light, it would be easier when and if it ended. Jen frowned as she didn't like thinking about that possibility, but knew she had to be realistic, too.

WHEN THEY ARRIVED HOME, FRANK WAS COMFORTABLY SETTLED at the kitchen table, sipping a root beer while Aunt Sorcha bustled around the kitchen.

"Something smells great," Ian said as they walked into the kitchen. "Hi, Frank."

"Meatloaf and mashies," Aunt Sorcha replied.

Pleasantries were exchanged and then Aunt Sorcha instructed them to join Frank at the table.

Jen helped Aunt Sorcha bring the food to the table and they all helped themselves, family style.

"What did you think of the condo?" Aunt Sorcha asked as she heaped potatoes onto her plate.

"It's stunning. I can see why Ian likes living there. The location is perfect."

"It looks like I'll be back there in another week or so."

"Well, you don't have to rush. We enjoy having you here, as long as you like." Aunt Sorcha didn't look happy about Ian moving out again and Jen found herself feeling the same. It was going to seem quiet without him there.

"Though I suppose we'll manage, won't we Jen?" she said cheerfully.

"Maybe I'll have all of you over to my place for dinner, once I'm settled back in again," Ian said.

Aunt Sorcha brightened at the invitation. "Oh, that would be marvelous. And I'm sure Frank would love to see your place, too. Right Frank?"

"Right, sure. Of course," Frank agreed as he poured gravy onto his meatloaf.

After they finished eating, Ian grabbed hold of Jen's hand under the table and smiled. "Jen, there's a movie I've been wanting to watch. Care to join me?"

"Sure," she agreed.

"You kids have fun. Frank and I are going to visit for a bit in the other room." Aunt Sorcha looked pleased that they were heading to Ian's apartment above the garage. Jen was glad that Ian had made the suggestion, to give them all a bit of privacy.

———

IAN'S APARTMENT AT HIS MOTHER'S HOUSE WAS A FAR CRY FROM his place in the city. It was cozy and comfortable, though. Just two small rooms, a tiny bedroom that had room for a double bed and not much else and the living room area that had a pull-out sofa, which is where Ella slept when she came to visit and there was also a matching club chair, a small coffee table and a big-screen TV that overpowered the room a bit, it was so large. Ian grinned when he saw her looking at it.

"That was my contribution. There was a much smaller TV, but I moved it into the bedroom. This bigger one was a necessity."

Jen chuckled. "Of course it was."

"Well, you have to admit, it is nice."

Jen nodded. He was right. It was, and once they were comfy on the sofa and Ian clicked on the TV, she could appreciate the huge screen. The movie that Ian wanted to watch was a romantic comedy that Jen had mentioned wanting to see as well. It was fun to watch, and Jen felt quite content as they snuggled on the sofa. Ian's arm was across her shoulder and she rested her head on his arm. Every now and then, he pulled her in for a quick kiss and it was overall a wonderful night. His phone dinged once, announcing a text message and Ian glanced at it, then set the phone back down without responding.

"Another work text. Nothing urgent ,though. It can wait until Monday," he said with a smile.

Jen sat up and looked at him with concern. "Well, I should hope so. You're supposed to be on vacation." A thought occurred to her. She hadn't seen Ian on his computer or phone at all for the whole week. But maybe he'd been working when she didn't see him. "Have you gotten many work calls or texts while you've been out?"

Ian chuckled. "Define 'many'."

"So, you've been working?"

Ian raised his eyebrows at her tone and hesitated a moment before choosing his words carefully. "I have not been working this week, but yeah, I've checked my emails and texts. It would be irresponsible for me not to."

"I see. And have you been replying back?"

"For the most part, no. But yeah, to a few of them, I have." He ran a hand through his hair and looked frustrated. "I own the company. I can't just ignore it completely."

"You could. If you wanted to. That's the whole point of a vacation." Her tone was frosty.

"For me, this was huge, and hard. I couldn't relax if I cut off all contact completely." He paused and then met her eyes. "The whole point of it is to relax, right? If I didn't check in, relaxing wouldn't be possible."

Jen yawned. "It's late. I think I'm going to head to bed. I'll see you and Ella tomorrow afternoon."

Ian took her hand and lightly ran his finger over her palm. His touch made her shiver, even though she was annoyed with him.

"You're not mad at me, I hope?" he asked softly.

"No, not mad. I'd just hoped you'd be able to have a real vacation."

He smiled. "This has been a great one. Relaxing. Wonderful." He leaned forward and lightly kissed her on the lips and then pulled back. "And special. Sleep well, Jen."

CHAPTER 25

T hanks for being flexible. I appreciate it," Nadine said when he picked up Ella.

"No problem. I'm off this week, so it's fine."

She looked at him in surprise. "You've been on holiday? All week?"

He chuckled. "Is that such a shock?"

"Well, frankly, yes." She narrowed her eyes at him. "What's going on with you? You don't go on holiday. Or at least you never used to."

"I know. I guess I was long overdue. We just closed a big deal, so the timing seemed good."

She didn't say anything to that. But he didn't expect congratulations, not from her.

"So, are you off doing something fun this weekend?" he asked.

She brightened at that. "We are, actually. We're off to the country to stay with friends for a surprise birthday party."

"Hi, Jen!" Ella called out when she saw Jen at the front door.

"How much longer is she staying for?" Nadine asked.

"I'm not sure. A few more weeks, maybe longer." Longer, he hoped, but figured it was wise to keep that comment to himself. As it was, Nadine was looking at him strangely.

"Right. Well, I should probably get going." She turned and climbed back into her SUV and a moment later was gone. Ian watched her go, then joined the others in the house.

"Daddy, Jen says we're going to have a picnic in the park!" Ella ran over to him, full of excitement.

"Does that sound like fun to you?" He pushed her hair out of her eyes as she smiled up at him.

"Yes, can we go right now?"

"Well, I was thinking we'd go tomorrow, but it is really nice and unusually warm. Maybe we could go today. What do you think, Jen?"

"I think it sounds like a great idea!"

"I can make you some sandwiches to take with you," his mother said. "I'd join you, but I'm meeting Gracie for bingo."

Jen helped Aunt Sorcha pack a picnic basket of food for them and they set off for the park soon after.

It wasn't a long drive, just fifteen minutes or so, and Ella seemed to know the area well.

"We'll go see the swans. Do you like swans, Jen?" His daughter's words came out in a rush, she was so excited about their little adventure.

"I think swans are beautiful," Jen answered.

When they arrived at the park, the sun was still shining brightly and the winds had calmed down so that it was a lovely, warm late afternoon. They started walking toward the pond and Ella ran ahead, then ran back to encourage them to walk faster.

"Hurry, we don't want to miss the swans."

"They're not going anywhere, dear," he assured her.

When they reached the pond's edge, Ella screamed with excitement when she saw the family of swans gliding across the water. There were seven of them—two bigger ones and five smaller, and they swam single file. They were a gorgeous sight to see.

"Daddy, there's more of them now. There were only three last time we came."

"That's right, dear. Should we have our picnic right here, then, so you can keep watching the swans?"

"Okay," she agreed.

Ian laid out the blanket his mother had given him to bring. It was a huge, soft green plaid and was plenty big enough for the three of them. Once they were settled, Jen opened the basket and drew out paper plates and bottled waters.

"Are you hungry yet, Ella? You could have a sandwich or some grapes to start? Or both?" Jen offered.

"Grapes!"

She handed her a small bunch of them and they ate their sandwiches as they relaxed and watched the swans swim by.

"Daddy, can I follow them?" Ella asked as she finished her sandwich.

"Stay along the edge, Ella, and come right back."

"I will." She scrambled up and they watched her skip along the edge of the pond, kicking up red and gold leaves as she went. The pond was small, so Ian wasn't worried that they'd lose sight of her, but still he kept a close watch as she ran around and then slowed to a stroll.

"She's having a good time," Jen said as she started to pack up their empty plates.

"She's always loved coming here," Ian agreed.

"I can see why. It's a beautiful spot," Jen said as she looked around. The park was busy but not too crowded, a mixture of families and couples enjoying a lovely fall day.

"I'm glad you came with us," he said as Ella came flying back over to them, holding something in her hand.

"Look what I have. It's a frog! A baby frog." She held her hand out so they could see the tiny creature.

"Very nice. Now go put him back in the pond. That's his home."

Ella pouted. "Do I have to? He's so cute. Can't I just bring him home with us?"

Ian shook his head and tried not to laugh. "Afraid not, dear. Back to the pond."

"Fine." She flounced off and Ian watched her go. A glance at Jen showed she'd been just as amused.

"She's very cute," Jen said.

"She is. I'm lucky," he agreed. He was feeling very lucky indeed and was a little surprised and pleased by how natural it felt to be there with both Jen and Ella. It was comfortable, as if they'd all been together for much longer. Had he ever felt this relaxed, this comfortable with Nadine?

"You look deep in thought," Jen commented.

Ian smiled. "I was just thinking how easy this feels. Like we've known each other much longer than we have."

"I know. It's taken me by surprise, a little," Jen admitted.

"Me, too." He reached for her hand and gave it a squeeze. "Do you have any idea how badly I want to kiss you right now?"

Jen chuckled. "Because you know that you can't. Not in front of Ella. Not yet."

"Right. Not yet. Too bad." He grinned. "Maybe we can tire her out with all this running around and she'll fall asleep early."

Ella came running over to them and Ian reluctantly let go of Jen's hand. He sensed that he needed to be very cautious about introducing Jen as anything more than a friend to his daughter.

But she apparently already had ideas.

"Daddy, are you going to marry Jen?"

The question nearly made him drop his bottle of water.

"Sweetie, Jen and I are just friends." He glanced at Jen and added, "Good friends, but we don't have any plans to get married."

"Okay." She looked quite serious, and then the moment passed. "Can I follow the swans again?" And she was off and running.

Ian shook his head as she went.

"Sorry about that."

"It's fine. She's six," Jen said sensibly.

"Well, at least she likes you, if she's already talking marriage!" he said and Jen laughed. He was glad, very glad, that Ella seemed to like her. He'd never introduced anyone that he'd dated to his daughter before as he didn't want to set the wrong expectation with anyone, but especially with his daughter. Yet, he'd been excited for her to meet Jen.

They stayed at the park for another hour or so, until they were all ready to head home. Ella was yawning as they got into the car and fell asleep halfway home. She woke up when they pulled into the driveway, and Ian helped her out of the car while Jen grabbed the picnic basket.

"Do you want to come up with us?" he asked Jen as they walked into the house.

"I don't think so. I don't want to take you away from her too much."

Ian was disappointed but also appreciated her consideration for Ella's feelings.

"Okay. What are you doing tomorrow?"

Jen's eyes lit up. "Your mother and I are going shopping and taking a drive out to a village I haven't seen yet."

"That sounds fun. Maybe we'll see you both for dinner tomorrow night?"

"I'm not sure. She mentioned meeting up with Gracie and someone else for dinner possibly."

"Oh, all right. Well, thanks for coming with us today. I think Ella likes you."

"She has good taste, obviously." Jen teased.

"Obviously," Ian agreed and watched as Jen walked towards her room.

CHAPTER 26

I'm so glad we're doing this," Aunt Sorcha said as they drove off the next morning to do some sightseeing. It was a lovely, sunny day, though the air was a bit cool and crisp. The village that she wanted to show her was about an hour's drive away and it was just as quaint as Jen had imagined. She took loads of pictures of the buildings and shops along main street to try and capture the feel of the area for her Pinterest board.

Aunt Sorcha's knees were a little stiff, so they took their time walking around, stopping every so often to explore a different store or sit to give her legs a rest. Around lunchtime, she introduced Jen to a tiny cafe that she'd once gone to and enjoyed. While they waited for their lunch, Aunt Sorcha chatted happily about all the plans that she and Frank seemed to have.

"We're going to visit his brother next Sunday. They live about an hour or so out of town and I haven't met them before. He doesn't see them as often as he'd like."

"It sounds like things are going well with Frank." Jen was glad to hear it. Aunt Sorcha's eyes lit up when she talked about him.

"It is funny, isn't it? We've been great friends for so long. I just didn't think of him that way. Until Lindy came along." Her eyes narrowed at the mention of the other woman.

Jen chuckled. "Sounds to me like she actually did you a favor. Opened your eyes to what was right in front of you."

Aunt Sorcha nodded. "That she did. I'd still prefer she kept her distance, though. She can set her sights on someone else."

Their soups came and the thick, fragrant split pea and ham was delicious. After they finished, they strolled across the street to a decadent bakery, where Aunt Sorcha selected a blueberry pie and a bag of fudgy brownies to bring home. The bakery was giving out samples of currant scones and they were so good that Jen bought a dozen of them. She'd grown quite addicted to scones during her time in Ireland.

They shopped a bit more and then made their way home to relax a bit before heading over to Gracie's house. Gracie was a wonderful cook, too, and they had a relaxing evening chatting over dinner.

"I'll teach you to make my scones before you go home," Gracie said when Jen asked her for the recipe. "There's a certain technique to handling the dough that's hard to explain on a recipe card. How much longer will you be here?"

Jen thought about that for a minute. The weeks were flying by. She had a return ticket booked and checked the date on her phone.

"Two weeks from tomorrow. It's going by so fast."

Aunt Sorcha furrowed her brow. "That seems awfully soon. Feels like you just got here. You're welcome to stay as long as you like. You could change your reservation."

"It's certainly tempting. But my family is expecting me back. There's a big party for my Uncle Jim's birthday and I always throw a holiday open house early in December."

"Does Ian know you're going back so soon?" Aunt Sorcha asked.

"I'm not sure if we've discussed the exact date. He knew, though, that I wasn't here for very long."

"I think he's gotten used to having you around." Aunt Sorcha looked sad. "We're both going to miss you."

Jen hated the thought of leaving, too. She knew these last two weeks would go by much too quickly.

"I'm going to miss all of you. I will have a talk with him, and remind him that I'm leaving soon."

"Good. Maybe you can work out something, a way to see each other again soon. I don't know how people do these long distance relationships."

"I know," Jen agreed. "It's going to be new to me, and probably him, too." By the time they got home it was past ten and all the lights were off in Ian's apartment. They all went to church Sunday morning and then back to the house for lunch. Jen relaxed in the afternoon, catching up on some reading and making notes for her next book. She said goodbye to Ella when she and Ian left later that afternoon to return her to her mother.

A few hours later, she heard him come in and thought he might want to visit for a bit, but when she wandered out to the kitchen, there was no sign of him.

"He's gone upstairs already. In for the night, I think," Aunt Sorcha said. She was sitting at the kitchen table thumbing through the Sunday paper. "He said something about getting ready for the week ahead."

"He's working?" Jen asked.

"Just getting ready to work."

"Same thing," Jen said and sighed.

"Why don't you have a slice of blueberry pie? And cut me one while you're there, would you? It's the one from the village bakery." That sounded like a good idea. Jen brought two dishes of pie to the table along with two forks and they both dug in.

"Oh, this is good." Jen was glad she'd cut herself a rather generous slice.

"Ian is missing out," Aunt Sorcha said with a wink as she took a big bite.

Jen chuckled. "Yes, he is."

CHAPTER 27

I missed you last week!" Merry said when Jen walked into the office the next day. Jen had to admit she liked working at an actual office and being around other people, especially Merry who had quickly become a good friend.

"It's nice to be back," Jen said. "Did we miss anything exciting?

Merry thought about that a moment. "No, not really. Everyone's just excited that that we landed the MacMurray business and busy getting going on it.

"Lunch today?" Jen asked as she reached her office door.

"Definitely. Max's on Monday. It's a tradition."

Jen got settled in her office, laptop fired up, her story open and ready to go. The only thing missing was a hot coffee. She went to the kitchen to get one and noticed Ian, already deep in conversation on his phone and someone waiting by his desk to talk to him. He looked swamped, and he'd just walked in the door. She supposed that was to be expected after coming off a week's vacation, though. She was glad that her own work was a bit calmer. Though she could tell Ian thrived on the energy of his work, it was just different.

Her morning went by quickly and she wrote several new chapters that seemed to pour out of her. It was often like that when she took a few days or a week even off in the middle of writing a book. Her mind was still working on it, so when she sat down to write, the ideas were all there. She looked up in surprise at a soft knock on her door. She'd been deep in the middle of a chapter and had lost all track of time.

"Are you ready to go?" Merry was standing there with her jacket on and purse in hand. Jen scrambled up from her desk and quickly shut her laptop off.

"I'm ready now."

Max's was packed, as usual. But it didn't take long for them to get through the line, get their salads and sit down to eat. They chatted easily as they ate and when they were just about done, Merry asked, "So, I can't stand it anymore…it's true, right? You and Ian are a thing now?"

Jen could feel her cheeks flush. "Is it that obvious?"

"Probably not to anyone else, except maybe Cal if you were to run into him. But I know you both and yeah, it's pretty clear to me."

Jen wasn't sure what to say to that, so she said nothing—which was fine because Merry wasn't done yet. "I think it's great. I haven't seen Ian like this about anyone else before." She frowned, though, and added, "But aren't you going home soon?"

Jen sighed. "Yes, too soon."

"Have you talked about what happens then? Have you had a long distance relationship before?"

"No, and no. We need to talk soon."

———

"YOU'RE GOING HOME IN TWO WEEKS?" IAN SET DOWN THE BOX of pizza on his coffee table. They had picked it up on the way home, as Aunt Sorcha was having dinner at Frank's house.

"Do you want some wine?" Jen asked as she poured herself a glass of merlot.

"Sure. Can't you push your ticket out? Stay longer? I know my mother wouldn't mind."

Jen brought the glasses of wine over to the sofa, sat down

next to Ian and reached for a slice. She'd been thinking about going home all afternoon, wondering if she might be able to stay longer. She'd even called the airlines and it would be a simple thing to push it out for another two weeks if she wanted to. She could get home a week before Uncle Jim's birthday.

"I might be able to extend it a little, for two weeks possibly."

"Well, that's better than nothing, I suppose."

"It's going by so fast," she said softly.

"Too fast," Ian agreed.

"Do you really think it can work? A long distance relationship?" She'd been thinking about that all afternoon, too. It seemed like such a huge hurdle.

But Ian was optimistic. "I don't see why not? We can make it work. You can come back to visit and I can take more time off, too. I've never been to Montana." He grinned and Jen leaned over and kissed him.

"Well, I would love to show you around."

THEY FELL INTO A ROUTINE OF SORTS, DRIVING INTO WORK together, then either having dinner with Aunt Sorcha or getting takeout and watching TV in Ian's apartment. Friday was the big moving day for Ian, and Jen's last day working in his office. It just didn't make sense once Ian moved out and wouldn't be driving in each day. Plus, as much as Jen enjoyed having lunch and coffee with Merry in the office, she didn't need to be there to get her work done. She could easily adapt to working out of Aunt Sorcha's living room or even the kitchen, like she often did at home.

She was looking forward to Friday night, too. Ian was planning to pack up the car with his stuff the night before—not that he had much stuff to speak of, mostly just clothes and his laptop. After work, they were going to have dinner at a steakhouse near the office then go back to his place to watch movies.

Ian wanted her to stay over, but she didn't feel right about that, not while staying at his mother's house, so he had reluctantly agreed to take her home eventually. They drove in earlier than usual on Friday, so Ian could stop by his apartment first, park the car and bring all his stuff in.

Merry insisted on taking her out to lunch on Friday and they made plans to go out the following week for after work drinks at the pub up the road from Aunt Sorcha's, the one that Tim had taken her to on her first night.

After work, they went to Crimson's, the steakhouse that Ian loved. It was just a block from the office and was full of business people, men in suits drinking martinis, elegantly dressed women sipping shimmering cocktails or glasses of wine. The lighting was dim and the seating was all black leather, soft and supple to the touch. The menu was extensive and the prices high.

"It's worth it," Ian said as she started to look over the menu. "Expensive, but the best steak I've had anywhere."

They ordered a bottle of cabernet and both got the porterhouse steak. The wine was rich and heavy and was even more delicious when the steak arrived, resting in a pool of butter.

Jen raised her eyebrow when she saw all the butter. As soon as the server walked away she said, "That is decadent."

Ian chuckled. "It sure is. Now take a bite."

She did, and sighed. "You're right. It's worth it." The butter and the wine complemented the steak perfectly.

"How often do you come here?" she asked. It was a dangerous place, too good.

"Not often enough. I take it you liked everything?"

"That is an understatement."

THEY SLOWLY MADE THEIR WAY BACK TO IAN'S CONDO. IT WAS about a ten-minute walk and it felt good to move around after eating such rich food. Jen had planned well, though, eating lightly at lunch so she could indulge at dinner.

They nodded at the doorman who smiled as they walked in

and got on the elevator. Ian took her hand as the elevator doors shut behind them. She felt a shift of energy in the air as he pulled her toward him and lowered his lips to hers. She lost herself in his kiss, barely noticing the whoosh of the elevator as they rode up. It wasn't until the movement came to a halt and the doors opened that either of them came up for air.

Ian let them into the condo and switched the lights on. They settled comfortably on the living room sofa and Ian clicked on the TV. They agreed on a movie, watched it for about two minutes and then it was completely forgotten as Ian pulled her into his arms. They kissed until they were both breathless and then Ian asked softly, "Do you want to go in the other room?" Jen nodded. It felt right and she'd been thinking about it all night. All week, if she was being honest.

Ian's bed was large and soft and they made good use of it. He kissed her softly and then wrapped his arms around her and held her close.

"That was amazing," he said. "I don't want you to go." He kissed her neck, and she sighed and stretched happily.

"We'll just have to make the most of the time we have left."

"I agree. Stay here tonight."

Jen was tempted. So tempted. But it didn't feel right. "If I wasn't staying with your mother, I wouldn't think twice. But I feel like I need to go back."

Ian brushed her hair off her face and kissed her forehead. "I understand. I don't like it, but I get it."

They stayed like that, wrapped in each others arms for a long while before they got dressed and Ian drove her home. He walked her to the door and kissed her thoroughly before saying, "See you tomorrow night. I'm cooking." He had invited his mother and Frank over to see the renovated condo.

"I'm looking forward to it." He waited until she was inside and then she watched him drive off. It certainly had been a night to remember and it was bittersweet that their time together was coming to an end.

CHAPTER 28

I t really looks wonderful, dear," his mother said the next evening as Ian gave them the grand tour. Frank looked suitably impressed but as was his way, didn't say much other than, "Nice place you got here." Which was fine with Ian. He'd always liked Frank and was glad that his mother seemed to be so happy. He'd loved his father, too, but five years was a long time to be single.

He kept sneaking glances at Jen. She looked absolutely gorgeous tonight in a pretty blue-green sweater dress that flattered her slim curves. They'd had a wonderful night the evening before, even better than he'd imagined it would be. Their chemistry was so strong and they got along so well. Ian wasn't used to things going so smoothly when it came to dating. It had been a long time since he'd even wanted to get serious about anyone. With Jen, it was different. Everything seemed better when he was around her.

"What's for dinner?" his mother asked as he led them into the dining room.

"I'm not very original, I'm afraid. The only thing I really know how to make is steak, so that's what we're having, with a salad I picked up at the market and baked potatoes. I hope that's all right?"

"It sounds good to me," Frank said.

"I'm sure it will be wonderful, dear. Can I help you with anything?"

"No, everything is done and keeping warm in the oven. We can eat now, if you're ready."

The steaks were a hit. After they finished eating, Jen helped him to clear the plates and then set out a platter of chocolate chip cookies while he made a pot of coffee.

"Did you make the cookies?" Frank sounded really impressed.

Ian laughed. "No, I got those at the market, too." He glanced at Jen and then at his mother. "Jen has some good news. She's going to extend her trip for a few weeks."

"You are? That's wonderful news!" She looked thrilled. Ian knew that his mother really liked Jen. She had never warmed up to Nadine, even after she had Ella, and his mother generally liked everyone.

"I think I can work it out to stay for two more weeks. As long as I make it home for Uncle Jim's birthday."

"How old will he be?" his mother asked.

"Ninety-three, I think, though you'd never know it. He has the energy of someone much younger. He tells me all the time that in his mind, he's still thirty-three."

His mother smiled. "That's a wonderful way to be, young at heart."

"He certainly is. Uncle Jim is quite a character. I miss him."

Ian reached for her hand under the table and gave it a squeeze. Jen met his eyes and smiled. Ian then noticed his mother watching the both of them.

"Ian, do you want to give Jen a ride back tomorrow? I think Frank and I are going to head out soon, before it gets too late. But I'm sure you young people want to visit a while longer."

Ian was stunned into silence. Jen looked at her nervously, "Are you sure?"

"Quite sure, dear. Frank are you ready to go?"

After they left, Ian turned to Jen and pulled her into his

arms. "You know what that was all about, don't you?" he asked.

"No. That surprised me, to be honest."

"I think my mother wants some alone time with Frank."

Jen's eyes grew wide. "Oh!"

"Not that I'm complaining, mind you." He was thrilled that Jen was going to be able to spend the night.

Jen laughed as he leaned in to kiss her.

"Shall we go make the most of the time we have left?"

CHAPTER 29

J en spent all day Sunday with Ian. It was a lovely, lazy day and she enjoyed every minute of it. They slept in, then Jen had fun puttering around Ian's kitchen, making omelets for brunch. They watched old movies, took a nap in the afternoon, ate leftovers for dinner and then around eight or so, he drove her home.

The following week was an adjustment, at first. The house felt quiet without Ian's presence and it also felt strange to not be going into the office. Jen was surprised to find that she missed the energy of people running around, and the friendly chatter of Merry as they shared their lunch and coffee breaks together. Aunt Sorcha was in and out and was careful not to bother Jen while she was hunched over her laptop writing.

By mid-week, she was looking forward to seeing Ian Wednesday night. He came by after work to take her to dinner. They went to another favorite restaurant near his condo and then back to his place after. Jen noticed that he'd been distracted at dinner, and his phone was buzzing constantly with text messages that he glanced at and occasionally answered.

"Is everything okay?" she'd finally asked when the waitress brought their dinners. Ian set his phone down and apologized.

"I'm sorry. We just had a client issue that needed to be resolved. Never a dull moment, you know."

Jen smiled. She knew how busy he was. "Is the new MacMurray project going well?"

"So far, so good. We are early stage, though. We'll be ramping up over the next few months as they get into their busy time."

"That sounds exciting," Jen said—though stressful was the word that actually came to mind.

"Most of the time, it's great," Ian agreed. "Until something goes wrong, and we have to put out fires."

"I'm glad I don't have to deal with that," Jen said, feeling grateful that when her characters misbehaved, she could usually get them back in line fairly easily.

Around ten, Ian dropped her off at Aunt Sorcha's.

"I'll see you on Saturday," he said as he gave her a lingering kiss goodbye. "Are you sure you don't want to just stay over Friday night? Stay the weekend?"

Jen was tempted, but it didn't feel right. "It's not that I don't want to, but I think it's too soon to do that to Ella. I don't want to confuse her."

Ian nodded. "I know you're probably right about that. Even though selfishly I want you to stay, too."

"There's always Sunday night," Jen said with a smile. They had talked about Ian swinging by when he dropped Ella off at her mother's Sunday night and then they'd be able to have some alone time, go out to dinner and relax for a while.

"Sleep tight," Ian said as she shut the car door behind her.

"ARE YOU EXCITED ABOUT YOUR WEEKEND AWAY?" JEN ASKED Aunt Sorcha the next morning over coffee. They were sitting at the kitchen table.

"I'm looking forward to it. But I'm a little nervous, too, I have to admit. It's been many years since I spent a whole weekend with a man, let alone a romantic get-away. Maybe I'm too old to be doing this."

Jen reached out and squeezed her hand reassuringly. "Don't be ridiculous. It's normal to feel nervous, a touch of the butterflies, at any age. I think it's wonderful and you're going to have a marvelous time."

"I hope you're right." She did seem calmer, though, as she broke off a piece of scone. "Frank's said the village we are going to is just lovely. Lots to do and see there."

"Good! Take loads of pictures so you can tell me all about it when you get back."

Aunt Sorcha furrowed her brow. "Are you sure you'll be all right here alone?"

Jen smiled. "Ian and Ella are coming by Saturday morning and we're going to spend the day together, and Friday night I'm looking forward to curling up on the sofa and watching old movies or maybe reading for a bit. I don't mind being alone at all, so please don't worry about leaving me."

"I guess I have no excuse not to go, then, do I?" Aunt Sorcha said with a chuckle.

"None at all," Jen agreed.

OVERALL, IT WAS A RELAXING WEEKEND. AS SHE'D MENTIONED to Aunt Sorcha, Jen followed through with her plan to stay in Friday night and watch old movies. She picked up a pint of mint chocolate chip ice cream and settled in to enjoy it. She also made a good dent in a new book she'd been meaning to read. This week away from seeing Ian all the time and going into the office had given her plenty of time to think and she was surprised by how much she was missing him. She'd grown used to their routine. She also realized that her feelings for him were growing stronger. And she still wondered how their relationship would fare once she went home to the States. She was trying not to think too much about that, though, and to instead enjoy the time they had left.

Ian came by with Ella around eleven Saturday morning

and they had a quick lunch at a local pizza shop before seeing an animated Disney movie that Ella loved. Like most Disney movies, it appealed to all ages and both Ian and Jen enjoyed it, and even though they'd just had lunch, they still treated themselves to buttered popcorn, too.

They had a wonderful day, and when they went back to Ian's condo, Ella put on a show for them, strutting around the living room and singing along to the radio until she got bored, and then they played various board games with her until it was time to start dinner. Ella said she wanted to help, so Jen gave her the job of tossing the salad, using a big set of tongs. She thought it was great fun and even managed to keep most of the salad in the bowl. After they all ate, Ian refused Jen's offer to help clean up.

"Go relax with Ella in the living room. It won't take me long to get everything put away."

"Will you read me a book?" Ella asked and tugged on Jen's arm to lead her over to the book case.

"Of course."

Ella picked out two of her favorite picture books and they settled on the comfy leather sofa. By the time Jen was halfway through the second book, Ian had joined them and Ella's eyes were drifting shut.

"Let's finish this tomorrow?" Ian said as he scooped up his sleepy daughter. He put her to bed and returned a few minutes later with a wicked gleam in his eye.

"So, there's one thing we didn't consider. I appreciate your view to not stay over while Ella is here…but, I can't leave her here alone and it doesn't seem right to put her in the car now that she's asleep, don't you think?"

Jen laughed. "Well, when you put it that way. I guess the responsible thing would be to stay over."

Ian flopped down on the sofa next to her. "I think it was a good day, overall."

"It was. She's a sweet girl. You're very lucky."

"I know." Ian leaned over and gave her a quick kiss. Then

he looked more serious as he asked, "When do you fly home, again?"

"Next Thursday. It's coming up fast."

"Well, we'll just have to make the most of the time we have left."

CHAPTER 30

Do you mind keeping an eye on Ella for a few minutes? I just have to send a quick email," Ian asked over breakfast the next morning as they sat around the kitchen table. He had cooked for all of them and his plate was already empty.

"Sure, no problem." Jen and Ella were only halfway through their meals. Twenty minutes later, they had finished up. Jen had rinsed the dishes and loaded them into the dishwasher and Ian was still in his office, with the door shut. Jen knew from how things were at his company that the closed office door meant not to disturb. Everyone in his office knew that. So, she led Ella into the living room and told her to pick out another book or two to read. It was almost an hour and three books later before Ian strolled into the room with a sheepish smile.

"I am so sorry. There's a bit of an issue at work and I lost track of time. Cal and I were emailing back and forth trying to come up with a solution."

Jen raised her eyebrow and knew her tone was frosty, but she couldn't help it. "Did you get it figured out?"

"Yes, I think so," he said carefully, as her tone registered. "You're mad, though. I'm really, really sorry. I promise it won't happen again." He made big puppy eyes at her and looked so damned cute that Jen couldn't stay mad at him.

"It's fine, really."

They went on to have a peaceful and relaxing day with Ella. They walked to a city park and Ella jumped in piles of colorful leaves that had gathered along the footpath. The wind was calm and the sun was shining, so that even though the air was cool, it was one of those lovely, crisp fall days where you could enjoy being outside.

Around four, they met up with Ella's mother for the drop-off and then Ian took her out for a relaxing Italian dinner. Both of them were conscious of time slipping away. They shared a bottle of wine and took their time, chatting over multiple courses. But eventually the dining room was mostly empty as was their bottle of wine and reluctantly, they left to go home. When Ian pulled into the driveway, the lights were mostly off, so he didn't come inside.

"Tell my mother I'll be joining you both for supper tomorrow."

"She'll love that."

JEN WAS UP FIRST THE NEXT MORNING AND WAS SIPPING COFFEE when Aunt Sorcha walked into the kitchen, looking sleepy.

"I can't believe I slept in," she said as she put a kettle on the stove for her tea.

"You had a busy weekend. Was it fun?" Jen settled at the kitchen table and glanced at the day's newspaper.

Aunt Sorcha joined her at the table as she waited for the water to boil.

"It was really nice. We had a wonderful time. Frank was right. It's a lovely village and we walked around most of it." She was beaming as she spoke and Jen was happy for her.

"I'm so glad things are going well for the two of you."

"Frank is easy to be with. He's always been a good friend,

and it just feels right. And special." The tea kettle whistled and she got up to fill her cup.

"Tell me about your weekend, dear. Did you and Ian have a nice time? It was his weekend with Ella right?"

Jen told her all about their weekend, leaving out the part where Ian abandoned them for over an hour to do work.

"Oh, and he said he's coming to dinner with us tonight."

"Oh, good. I've got a hankering to try out a new recipe I ran across."

"Merry said to tell you hello," Ian said over dinner.

"Oh, how is she? I miss seeing her." Aunt Sorcha's new chicken recipe was a winner. Ian had raved about it, and his mother had seemed thrilled to hear it and to tell Ian all about her weekend away.

"She's good. She suggested that we all go out for drinks Wednesday night before you go away, if that sounds good to you. Just right after work. We can go have a nice dinner after."

"That sounds great. I'd love to see her and the others again before I leave." Jen had been feeling a little down all day at the thought of leaving so soon, and the suggestion cheered her up. She only had two more nights left before she was due to fly back. Aunt Sorcha and Merry were taking her to lunch tomorrow and Ian said he'd be by after work again so they could have dinner at his place and spend some time together.

After they finished dinner and chatted for a bit with Aunt Sorcha over coffee and dessert, Jen walked Ian out to his car. He pulled her in close and kissed her goodbye.

"Two nights left. I'll be by around the same time tomorrow, a little earlier if I can manage it, and we'll have a nice dinner at my place, unless you'd rather go out?"

"Staying in sounds perfect to me," Jen said happily.

CHAPTER 31

Jen woke Wednesday morning feeling unsettled. It was her last day in Ireland and she knew it was going to feel like the day was on fast forward. She stretched in bed and checked the time on her cell phone. It was almost seven. She could relax for another five minutes or so before heading to the kitchen for coffee and a chat with Aunt Sorcha. She'd be up by now, and was probably sipping her tea and reading the morning paper.

Jen was looking forward to seeing Merry and the others from Ian's company for after work drinks. It would be fun to catch up, and she sensed that even when she went back to the States that she'd still keep in touch with Merry. They had already connected on Facebook and had exchanged emails. In some ways, the world was a small place, she thought, not for the first time. With her writing, she'd made online friends all over the world. They kept in touch mostly through Facebook, but she also met up with quite a few at various writer conferences which was always fun, and she'd become very close friends with several. They often made plans to visit each other once or twice a year, schedules permitting.

Ian had said as much the night before as they'd been snuggling in his bed. Her feathers had been ruffled earlier in the evening when instead of picking her up early, he had lost track of time at work and was running late instead. He was full of apologies though, and promised to make it up to her and to visit as soon as he could.

"Maybe I can get there over the holidays at some point. I've never been to Montana. And you can come back in the spring, or sooner."

"I'd love to have you visit." She smiled and ran a hand through his thick, tousled hair, smoothing it back into place.

"And maybe I'll even get on Facebook, so I can at least see you there. I've resisted it up to now, though the company has a page."

"You really should be on Facebook. Even your mother and Frank are on it," she had teased him.

The night had flown by, and too soon, it was time for Ian to drive her home.

"Merry emailed me earlier today. She said you told her she could leave early. She's going to swing by and pick me up, so we can get to the pub and chat a bit before everyone gets there. That was nice of you."

Ian smiled. "I know she misses having you in the office. There's not many women there, in case you didn't notice."

Jen chuckled. "It will be fun to see them all again. I didn't think I was going to like working there as much as I did. It was a nice mix of quiet when I closed my door and people if I got up to walk around. I'll miss that."

"Maybe you can find another company that has a spare office," Ian had teased, but Jen was already seriously considering the idea. There were shared office spaces where smaller companies or individual workers like her could rent an office.

MERRY CAME BY TO PICK HER UP AT A FEW MINUTES PAST FIVE and ten minutes later, they were comfortably situated at the bar at MacGregor's. Merry was sipping a pint of Guiness and Jen had a glass of merlot.

"Did you do anything fun on your last day here?" Merry asked.

"Ian's mother and her best friend Gracie took me out to lunch, and we walked around and did a little shopping. I picked up a few gifts for family back home. It was nice. Bittersweet, though. I'm going to really miss them both."

"You'll be back, though, for visits? It's not too long of a plane ride?"

Jen laughed. "It's a full day of traveling. Three planes, no direct flights."

Merry made a face. "Ugh. I don't envy you that. I hate flying."

"I'm not a fan of it, either. But it's worth it."

Merry was quiet for a moment and then looked more serious. "Do you think that you and Ian will be able to make it work? I've never had a long-distance relationship."

Jen took a sip of wine. "I never have, either. I have to admit, the distance does worry me."

"Well, if it's meant to be, it will work. My fingers are crossed for you both."

"Thanks." They spent the next forty-five minutes catching up. Merry filled her in on her latest big project and asked her advice. She and her husband were renovating a fixer upper they'd bought and had just put their own house on the market.

"We're hoping to juggle the timing so that we can move into the new place and close on the other soon after. But we're prepared in case it doesn't sell right away. It's a little stressful, though."

"I can imagine." Jen remembered the stress of buying her own condo. As a writer, she was self-employed and there had been so many more hoops to jump through before the bank would agree to give her a mortgage.

Half a dozen other employees arrived—Cal and his wife, Jane and some of the engineers on the team. They all stopped by to wish her well, and Cal bought them both another round of drinks. Whenever the door opened, Jen glanced over to see if it was Ian walking in, but it never was. She started to worry a bit when three more engineers walked in and one of them mentioned that Ian's door was closed.

"You don't think he's still at work, do you?" she asked Merry, who looked uncomfortable, too, at the mention of the closed door.

"It was closed when I left, but that was early, a little past four. I wouldn't think he'd still be there, but everyone knows not to bother him when his door is shut." She took a sip of her beer and then added, "Maybe you should text him. He sometimes loses all track of time if he's focusing on something."

Jen pulled out her phone and texted Ian. "Are you on your way?"

A minute later her phone dinged with a reply. "I am now. I'm sorry, got hung up on something. I'll be there as soon as I can."

"He's on his way," she told Merry, feeling sick inside. Her last night in Ireland and he forgot?

"I'm sure he feels terrible about it," Merry said. She seemed to sense that Jen was upset, and changed the subject.

"So, I need your advice on colors. We're torn between a few shades of gray. Some have more of a blue tone to them. What do you think?" She pulled out three paint swatches and Jen tried to focus on them instead of the fact that she was at a bar with Ian's friends and colleagues and he was going to be well over an hour late. All the original doubts she'd had about his workaholic ways resurfaced. Was this a sign of how it would be or worse? She began to feel like a fool for thinking they could make this work.

She laughed and joked with Merry, Cal and his wife Jane, and the other engineers and when Ian came rushing in, full of apologies, she simply smiled and acted as though she didn't mind at all, even though she was seething inside. She didn't want to make a fuss in front of his friends, especially as she really did enjoy their company and thought it was thoughtful of them to meet her for drinks and wish her well.

"I got here as soon as I could. Luckily, the traffic wasn't too bad," Ian said as he settled into a bar seat that opened on Merry's left.

"It's fortunate that traffic was light," she said with a tight smile.

"Did I mention how sorry I am that I ran late? We just have this problem and I finally figured out a solution. I was working on it all afternoon." His eyes pleaded for her to understand.

"That's really great. I'm happy for you." Jen turned to Merry and asked her to tell her more about her plans for the kitchen renovation. Her back was to Ian, but he was surrounded by Cal and the engineers and was quickly drawn into their conversation. After about an hour, people started to drift out. Merry threw her arms around Jen and gave her a tearful goodbye hug.

"I'm going to really miss you! Message me when you get home, so I know you made it there safely," she demanded.

"I will," Jen agreed and felt tears well up, too. She was feeling emotional, especially now that it was just the two of them left at the bar.

"Are you ready to grab a bite to eat?" Ian asked as he stood and signed the credit card receipt.

"Sure," Jen said with little enthusiasm.

Neither of them spoke as they drove the short distance to a restaurant that they'd been to before. Jen wasn't overly hungry but knew she should eat something. She ordered a bowl of lamb stew and a glass of water.

"Nothing else to drink for you?" Ian sounded surprised as he put in his order for a pint and a burger.

"I've had enough, and have a long day tomorrow."

"Right. Did you still want to come back to my place tonight? It is our last night together." He sounded uncertain and Jen knew he'd picked up that she was not happy with him. She didn't feel mad anymore, though, just a heavy sadness as it became clear to her what she needed to do.

"I don't think so. When you forgot about meeting us tonight, I had some time to really think, before you finally showed up. You know my original concern about dating a workaholic? It's who you are, and I think we might be better off to just call it quits now. I'll go back to Montana, you can go back to work and we'll both just move on."

Ian looked stricken. He reached out and grabbed one of her hands.

"You're just upset. And I don't blame you. I can work on that, though. You already got me to take a break, remember?"

Jen smiled sadly. "Right. But you've reverted back to the way you were. You did it last night and the other day with Ella, too. Tonight just made it even more clear. It's not going to work with us. We're too different. I don't know how a long distance relationship would work anyway with us being this far apart. It's not realistic for either of us."

"We could make it work!" Ian tried again as the waitress returned with their food. They both ate in uncomfortable silence. Jen's appetite was gone and she only had a few bites of the stew. She was dangerously close to tears and feeling miserable.

"I know you're upset with me. But don't give up totally. I really think we could make this work."

"I honestly don't see how." Jen took a final bite and pushed the bowl away. The waiter cleared the table and brought the check over. Ian pulled out some cash, set it down and they left. Five minutes later, he pulled up to his mother's house.

"I'm still planning to drive you to the airport tomorrow. I'll be here at six to get you."

"You're sure? I could take a cab, or have your mother drive me." Jen thought it would be too hard for both of them to have Ian drive her.

A muscle jumped in his jaw. "I'm sure. I'll see you tomorrow. Good night, Jen."

"Good night," she said softly as she opened the door. She'd been looking forward to this night and it had ended very differently than she'd imagined.

CHAPTER 32

Jen was exhausted when her alarm went off the next morning at five sharp. She'd slept fitfully and it had been at least an hour before she finally drifted off to sleep. She showered quickly and dressed, and did a last minute check to make sure she had everything packed. Aunt Sorcha had a cup of coffee ready for her when she joined her in the kitchen and Jen didn't have the heart to tell her that she'd ended things with Ian. He could do that. She wanted their last morning together to be as cheerful as she could manage.

"I can't thank you enough for letting me stay with you these past few months," she said as she gratefully reached for the hot coffee.

"It's been my pleasure having you here. The house is going to seem quiet when you go."

Jen smiled. "You have Frank to keep you company now."

Aunt Sorcha's eyes lit up. "I do, that's true. He's coming over for dinner tonight."

"Meatballs?" Jen asked. Aunt Sorcha often made a batch of meatballs when she had company coming.

"It might be. Frank seems to love my meatballs," she said happily.

Jen finished her coffee just as they heard Ian's car pull into the driveway.

"Is it time to go already?" Aunt Sorcha said, looking at the clock. It was a minute before six. Jen put her empty cup in the dishwasher and went to her bedroom to get her luggage. She turned when she heard Ian's footsteps coming down the hall.

"I'll get those for you." He met her eyes for a minute, then reached for her bags and headed out the front door with them. Jen and Aunt Sorcha followed and Jen gave his mother a big hug. "Thanks again. I'm going to miss you!"

"You promise to keep in touch? You've got my email address?"

"I do, and I will," Jen confirmed as she and Ian climbed into the car. She waved goodbye to Aunt Sorcha as Ian drove off.

"How are you feeling this morning?" he asked once they were on the highway.

"I'm tired. I didn't sleep great last night." She knew he was asking if she still felt the same and she did. When she woke it was with a heavy sadness but also sureness that she was making the right decision. After breaking up with Paul for the reasons that she did, it didn't make sense to stay with someone who seemed to have the same issues. It didn't make her feel any better, though.

"Did you have a chance to think about us?" he asked.

"I haven't changed my mind. I'm sorry, Ian." She expected him to try and talk her out of it but he didn't. He just sounded tired and resigned.

"Fine. Maybe you're right." Okay, that stung. She glanced at him and he was unsmiling and serious.

"I've done some thinking, too, about what you said. Maybe it's just not meant to be."

"Right, okay." Jen felt even worse knowing he apparently agreed with her way of thinking, but she supposed it must be for the best. Better to end it now and try to just remember the happy times. She sighed, thinking that he'd gotten what he said he wanted after all, a holiday fling.

IAN HAD HOPED THAT JEN WOULD HAVE COOLED DOWN AND reconsidered ending things after a good night's sleep, but she seemed even more determined. The sadness in the air was a tangible thing and it was frustrating. Ian wasn't used to things not going his way and he didn't like it. What he said was true, though. He'd barely slept the night before, either, and had thought a lot about what Jen had said. If it was so easy for her to end things, to not even try further, then maybe what they had wasn't as strong as he'd thought it was.

He reminded himself that he hadn't been looking to get serious with anyone, so really it should be a relief that she'd come to this decision. They could both move on and remember each other fondly. So why then did he have what felt like a huge empty ache, an oppressive weight of sadness? Maybe it was because it had been a very long time since he'd been in this position, the one who was being dumped. It wasn't a good feeling.

When they reached the airport, he pulled up to the curb and got Jen's bags out for her. They were both on wheels, so she could check them in outside.

"So, this is it, then. I will miss you, Jen."

"I'll miss you, too," she sniffed and her eyes were glistening.

He pulled her in for a tight hug and a tender, sweet kiss.

"Have a safe trip home. I hope you don't mind if I call sometime to say hello? See how my Montana friend is doing?"

She looked confused. "Okay, sure. Of course. Give my best to your mother and I didn't say anything to her, so if you don't mind…"

"I'll talk to her. Bye, Jen."

He watched her walk off, with her coat wrapped tightly around her, her purse slung over her shoulder and her bags trailing along behind her. A porter came rushing over and took them from her, and she turned back and gave him a small wave goodbye. She looked as sad as he felt and he sighed as he got back into his car and drove off.

CHAPTER 33

I t felt good and comforting to be home. Jen spent the first week back writing up a storm and trying unsuccessfully not to think of Ian. She'd mentioned him to her sister, Isabella, in her emails home, but hadn't let anyone except Mandy know that she'd actually started a relationship with him.

After two days of battling jet lag and dropping in on family members to say hello, she had holed up for the rest of the week and tried her best to lose herself in her story. She was at the point, in the final quarter, where it was easy to do that. She lost all track of time as the hours flew by and she gave her characters the heartfelt, satisfying ending that she'd dreamed of for herself. It was both cathartic and depressing at the same time.

Her doorbell rang as she finished editing a chapter and she realized it was already five o'clock. Mandy was stopping by for an after-work drink before they headed to her mother's house for Uncle Jim's birthday party.

"I brought a bottle of La Crema," Mandy said as she walked into the kitchen and found the wine opener. It was their current favorite chardonnay, creamy and buttery, and Jen gratefully accepted a cold glass of it.

"Thank you," she said as Mandy cocked her head and took a good look at her.

"You look terrible. Are you coming down with something?" she asked as she took a step back.

"Thanks. Not that I know of. I feel fine, just tired. I'm always tired lately," Jen joked.

"Maybe that's it. You look a little pale." Mandy settled onto one of the stools at the island, and Jen joined her and took a sip of the wine, appreciating it's cool comfort.

"Are you sure you're okay?" Mandy asked.

"I'm fine," Jen assured her.

"Is it Ian? Have you heard from him?"

Jen sighed. "No, not a word."

"Oh, is that the problem, then? Did you expect to?"

Jen considered the question. "No. Maybe. I don't know. It was my idea to end things, but he seemed to agree when he took me to the airport. I guess I didn't expect to miss him so much."

"Really? Are you saying it was easier when you broke up with Paul? After dating for a year?" Mandy looked intrigued.

"Yes. I was sad when it ended with Paul, but I didn't miss him as much. Not like this. Crazy, huh? Missing someone that I'm not in a relationship with who is in another country. No wonder I'm still single."

"Don't be so hard on yourself. At least you had someone, even if it was for a short while. I'm completely and totally single. I haven't had a single date since you left."

Jen looked at her friend and shook her head. Mandy was gorgeous. If she wasn't dating, it was her choice.

"You could be dating someone if you wanted to," Jen said quietly.

Mandy sighed. "I suppose so. It's just easier sometimes to do nothing. To wait for tomorrow but then before you know it, a few months of tomorrows have gone by."

"You just weren't ready."

"Maybe not," Mandy agreed. "But we're not talking about me. Do you love him?" The shift caught Jen by surprise.

"Ian?"

"Who else?" Mandy said with a chuckle.

"I don't know. We never said it, either of us. Neither of us was looking to fall in love."

"So, you don't love him?" Mandy pressed. There was a long moment of silence as Jen thought about the question, not for the first time. It was something she'd been thinking about a lot lately.

"Maybe I do, or did. What a mess." Did she love Ian? It would certainly explain why she was so miserable. It didn't change anything, though. The same issues were still there.

"If you love each other, maybe you can find a way to make it work. Just saying," Mandy said.

"I don't think so. We both made the same choice. I'm sure I'll feel better in time. It's just recent and raw."

"And it's the holidays," Mandy agreed. "An easy time of year to feel blue anyway if you're alone. I can't believe Thanksgiving is two days away. And then your party a week from this Saturday. That should get you into the holiday spirit."

"It usually does," Jen agreed with a smile. She always looked forward to her annual Christmas party. It was like a big open house, with friends and family, lots of good food and fun.

"How's Uncle Jim? His ninety-third, right?"

"Yes, he's amazing. Being around him always puts me in a good mood. We should head over."

AN HOUR LATER, JEN AND MANDY, ISABELLA, THEIR MOTHER and Tom, Uncle Jim and several of his friends were enjoying a festive birthday dinner.

After everyone had eaten and had cake and coffee, Uncle Jim pulled Jen aside and looked her in the eye.

"You're not yourself. Did you go and fall in love with an Irishman?" He was teasing her, but his eyes were soft and worried.

"Sort of," Jen admitted. "We broke things off when I left. He was a workaholic, like Paul, and I couldn't do that again.

And he's in another country. Two big issues. He agreed it was smart to call it a holiday fling."

Uncle Jim looked doubtful. "Really? Well, the world gets smaller all the time, my dear. So that's not really an issue. Maybe it didn't work with that Paul because he wasn't the one for you. Seems to me that you could probably fix that other issue if you both want to. What do I know, though? I'm just an old man," he joked.

"You seem pretty smart to me," Jen said.

Uncle Jim looked serious as he took her hand and gave it a squeeze.

"I think it's time I told you about my Elena." He paused for a moment and smiled sadly before continuing. "She is the one that got away. We met in Germany many, many years ago. I wanted to marry her then, but she couldn't leave her family and I was foolish and refused to stay there. I regretted it, of course, and a few years later, I wrote to her and said I was ready to do it, to move abroad, but it was too late. I'd waited too long, and of course, someone much smarter than me had the good sense to marry her."

"Is that why you never married?" Jen asked softly.

He nodded. "There was only one Elena. No one ever compared to her. I just don't want you to make the same mistake I did. Be happy."

She leaned over and kissed his cheek. "Thank you, Uncle Jim. I'll think about what you said."

CHAPTER 34

The next day, after a delicious and wonderfully relaxing Thanksgiving dinner with the family, Jen returned home to her condo, which felt empty and quiet in comparison, but soothing, too. She changed into sweats, and curled up on her living room sofa with a fleece throw and her laptop. She jumped up first, and turned the heat up a little as the temperature had dropped that afternoon when the winds picked up and suddenly it felt chilly. When she settled back onto the sofa and opened her laptop, she had several emails, and smiled to see that one was from Merry and then her breath caught when she saw there was one from Ian, too.

She opened Merry's email first. It was a chatty note, wishing her a Happy Thanksgiving and then mentioning that Ian had been a bear to work with ever since she left.

"Have you heard from him? He's been moping around the office looking like someone died and he's no fun to work with at all. I hope you don't mind, but I suggested he write you, and at least say hello. Maybe that will cheer him up? I hope things are going well for you? I miss you!"

Interesting. So maybe Ian was missing her a little? Nervously, she clicked on his email next, wondering what he would have to say. His message was short, and sweet.

"Hi, Jen,

Well, I just wanted to say hello and Happy Thanksgiving. I know that's a big holiday for you. Just wanted to let you know I was thinking of you. I hope you're doing well.

Ian

She smiled as she reread the message. It wasn't a declaration of love, but if he was thinking of her, maybe that meant he was missing her, too. She wrote back quickly, before she lost her nerve.

"Hi Ian,

Thank you. It's great to hear from you. It was a wonderful day. We all went to my mother's house for dinner and we celebrated my Uncle Jim's 93rd birthday too.

I know you mentioned possibly coming to visit over the holidays? I know this is last minute and maybe it doesn't make sense for you, given our last conversation, but if you're able to get away, I'm including an invite to my Christmas party a week from Saturday.

Cheers,

Jen

She attached the colorful graphic with snowflakes and party information, including her address and directions. She hit send and then immediately felt silly. There was no way he'd want to come now or even be able to do it on such short notice. He was probably buried with work, and she was just caught up in the moment and feeling sentimental. She yawned, suddenly feeling very tired. Given the time difference, she wasn't likely to hear back from either Merry or Ian for hours. Time for bed.

The following morning, Jen had a reply from Merry, but no word from Ian. Oh, well. She got busy on her day and lost herself in editing until noon when her stomach growled and she noticed the time. She stretched and went to the kitchen to heat up some Thanksgiving leftovers that her mother had sent her home with. She'd just finished a hot turkey sandwich with gravy and was about to dive back into editing when her phone rang and she was surprised to see that it was an international number, Ian.

"Hello?"

"It's Ian." It was so good to hear his voice.

"How are you?"

"I got your email and your invitation. You're serious?" He sounded uncertain.

"I know you're probably too busy. It's okay. I know it's last minute," she apologized. He was quiet for a moment, then said, "No, I'd love to come. I have to move some things around, but I think I can do it. How've you been?"

"Good. Working a lot, keeping busy."

Jen heard voices in the background and the sound of another phone ringing.

"Someone's looking for me. I should go. I'll see what I can do. I'd love to see you," he said.

"I'd love to see you, too. Bye, Ian."

Jen hung up the phone and felt happy for the first time since she'd come home. She was on cloud nine for the next few days, until the glow faded when she hadn't heard from Ian and realized it must mean he wasn't coming.

Sure enough, a text message came in from him that

evening. "Still trying to move a meeting, but it doesn't look good. I'm sorry. If anything changes will let you know, but best to count me out this time."

Jen felt her eyes well up as her hope dimmed. Once again, work came first. She knew it was last minute but still, he owned the company. Surely meetings could be changed? But then she thought of Jim MacMurray and other key clients that they walked on eggshells for. Business was business, she supposed. Maybe she had been foolish to think they had a chance.

WHEN FRIDAY CAME AND THERE WAS NO UPDATE FROM IAN, JEN knew the last minute visit wasn't going to happen. So when she accidentally dropped her phone in a sink full of water late that afternoon, she just laughed and stuck it in a bag of rice to dry out. It wasn't the first time she'd done that and usually after a day or two submerged in rice, they came back to life. She had a land line, so if anyone needed to reach her, they could call that number.

She went back to the sink, and finished washing and peeling the vegetables she was preparing for her tray of veggies and dip. She liked to have as much of the prep work done ahead of time so there was less to do the day of the party. Plus, most of her friends were going to be bringing their favorite appetizers, so there would be plenty of food.

CHAPTER 35

The first guests arrived a little past four. Jen had chips and dip and veggie trays on the island, along with her famous taco dip and sausage-stuffed meatballs. Mandy brought a platter with assorted cheese and crackers and before long, her dining room table was overflowing with various appetizers. The wine and cocktails were flowing and all of her friends and family were there. Jen smiled as she overheard Uncle Jim chatting to Mandy. She opened another bottle of wine and poured a glass for Isabella who had just arrived.

"Are you expecting anyone to be coming by cab?" Isabella asked as Jen handed her the wine.

"By cab? No, why?"

"A taxi was pulling up as I walked in. Maybe they were going to a different condo?"

Jen walked to the door, feeling her pulse race. Was it possible? It couldn't be. As she reached the door, there was a knock, and she opened it. Ian stood there, carrying a leather bag, and smiling as fluffy snowflakes fell around him.

"I tried to call, but I couldn't get through. Is something wrong with your phone?"

"I dropped it in water. I didn't think you were coming." She suddenly felt shy. Ian grinned and pulled her towards him. She shut the door behind her and they were both alone on the front steps.

"I missed you," he said simply as he leaned in to kiss her. His lips felt wonderful on hers and she didn't want to stop kissing him, but knew they had to go inside and that there would be questions. Her heart was still racing and she felt ridiculously happy.

"I missed you, too. So much. Come in, and meet everyone." Jen took his bag and set it in the front hall closet as they walked in. She opened a beer for him and then introduced him to her family, most of whom were gathered around her kitchen island, nibbling on snacks and trying not to look like they were all dying of curiosity to meet her visitor. As she'd predicted, he and Uncle Jim hit it off immediately. While they were busy chatting, Mandy pulled her aside.

"I haven't seen Ian since he was maybe twelve or so. You never mentioned how adorable he was. And that accent! I may need to plan a trip to Ireland."

"I have to admit, I love listening to him talk."

"Have you noticed people always say that about foreign accents…but never American ones?"

Jen laughed. "That's very true. People recognized my accent as American, but no one said they liked it!" They walked back over to where Ian and Uncle Jim were deep in conversation. Both looked up when they saw them. A mischievous gleam came into Uncle Jim's eyes. "I was just asking Ian here how far Dublin is by plane. Maybe I will pop over for a visit."

"I'll go with you," Mandy said with a smile. "I'd love to see Aunt Sorcha. It's been too long. It's really great to see you." She gave Ian a big hug.

"I know she'd love to see you both." Ian grinned. "Mandy, last time I saw you, you were just a kid."

"I know. I was just telling Jen I wouldn't have even recognized you, it's been so long."

They all chatted for a few more minutes and then Jen turned her attention back to Ian.

"Are you tired? It was more than a few hours on planes for you." Jen knew Ian's day had been a long one. It was past midnight in Ireland.

"It hasn't really hit me yet. I slept some and got a second wind once we landed. Or maybe it's nervous energy. It crossed my mind when I didn't hear from you that maybe you'd changed your mind about wanting me to come."

Jen put her hand on his. "I'm so sorry about that. When I dropped the phone in the water, I just assumed that you weren't coming at that point. But, I didn't change my mind. I'm glad you're here."

The rest of the evening seemed to fly by, though Jen guessed that the time difference must have caught up with Ian. By the time everyone cleared out, around eleven, he looked exhausted. Mandy and Isabella had stayed to help her clean up, so there wasn't much left to do after they left. As soon as the door shut behind them, Ian pulled her toward him and led her to the living room sofa.

"Finally, we're alone," he said softly.

"You must be ready to drop."

"I'm tired, but there's a few things I need to say to you. Your family is great, by the way."

"Thanks. I think they're pretty special, and they liked you, too."

Ian leaned back, put his arm around her and pulled her toward him, so she was facing him. With his other hand, he took hers and gave it a gentle squeeze, then slowly ran his thumb along her palm, which gave her the shivers.

"Since you left, I've had a lot of time to think, and the time apart has made me realize how important you are to me. I've missed you more than I ever imagined that I would. Even when I moved home to my condo I was missing you then, too, but I didn't understand it at the time. I missed seeing you at the end of every day. My happiest days were when you came into work with me, knowing you were right down the hall, riding to and from the office and just chatting about every day stuff. I've missed sharing all of that with you."

"I've missed that, too. I've missed you more than I thought I would, to be honest," she admitted.

Ian smiled. "This is new territory for me. I was used to doing what I wanted, whenever I wanted to do it. Working all hours was normal and just what I did. But then you came along and changed that. I realized that working as much as I did was actually selfish, if I wanted to spend time with you, too."

Jen said nothing. She agreed with him, but just gave his hand a squeeze and after a moment, he continued.

"So, I've been thinking, a lot, about how we could make this work."

Jen smiled and realized she'd been holding her breath, still nervous about where they would go from here. She hoped that he might want the same thing that she did.

"I talked to Merry first, ran my idea by her. She approves, by the way." He grinned and Jen laughed.

"So spill it, already. What are you proposing?"

"Well, first of all, I know we've only known each other a few months and maybe it seems like we are rushing things, but I think it's true what some people say. When you know, you just know."

Jen nodded in agreement.

"I talked with Merry, as I said, and we have a new rule now. About my closed door. It still means do not disturb... unless it's you. I told her that I need her help with that. If we have plans, she'll know my schedule and know to interrupt me if she needs to, to make sure I'm never late for you. And I can trust you to keep me in line at home, especially when Ella is around."

Jen felt a wave of joy sweep over her.

"Thing is, I'm at the point now with the business that I can step back and delegate more. I think you mentioned that and you're right. I don't have to go to every meeting. I wasn't able to reschedule a meeting for today that was important, but I sent someone else, filled him in and am trusting him to represent us well. I need to do that more."

"I'm glad to hear it," Jen said happily.

Ian chuckled as he reached into his back pocket. "Oh, and it's funny you should mention the word, proposing…" He pulled out a small, black velvet box, and opened it. Jen gasped. The diamond ring inside was exquisite—large but not overly so, square cut and surrounded by tiny diamonds in an elegant, filigree setting, with a vintage look. His voice wavered a bit as he started talking.

"I practiced this in my head over and over again on the plane, but each time the words were different, so I'm just going to speak from my heart and I'm no poet, but it's this simple. I love you, Jen. I've never felt like this about anyone before and I want to plan a life together. These past few weeks apart have been hard, and I've missed you more each day. Is there a chance that you feel the same?"

Jen answered by pulling him toward her and kissing him, while tears welled up and spilled over. But this time they were happy ones.

"Yes. I feel the same. It took me by surprise. I didn't expect this to happen."

Ian laughed. "I didn't, either. So, you're saying yes? You'll marry me?"

"Yes, of course I'll marry you." He slid the ring on her finger and they both stared at it.

"It's beautiful, and it fits. How did you know?" Jen couldn't take her eyes off it.

"It was my grandmother's ring. My mother gave it to me for you. She approves, too, by the way."

"She knows?"

"She was thrilled, and hopeful. She said the ring was too small for her but that your hands seemed about the same size, but a little smaller, so she knew it would be close. We can get it sized if we need to."

Jen put her hand over the ring and twisted it around. "I'm never taking it off. It fits perfectly."

"Good! So, lets talk logistics then. How soon can you come back to Ireland?"

Jen was quiet for a moment, thinking, and Ian rushed to add. "I know it's going to be hard for you to leave your family, but we can come back every few months or so for a week at a time and you can stay longer if you like, of course, and I was thinking maybe in the summer we could stay for a month or so. I could work remotely. Nadine and I had talked about splitting the summer and each taking Ella for a full month, so we could bring her here."

"That would be wonderful, for her and for us."

"So, it's settled, then." He took her hands and kissed her again, and she sank into him, happier than she'd ever been before.

EPILOGUE

A TALL, beautifully decorated Christmas tree twinkled merrily in the corner of Ian's living room. Ella was stretched out below it, thumbing through a gift from Jen, the latest *Fancy Nancy* picture book. Jen had always thought those books were adorable and was glad that Ella was enjoying the adventures of the spunky heroine, who loved to dress up. It was getting late, though, and Ella didn't protest too loudly when Ian led her off to bed. Jen went, too, to help tuck her in.

"Happy New Year, Ella!" she said as the little girl yawned and allowed Jen to set her book on the nightstand.

"Are we still going ice-skating tomorrow?" Ella asked sleepily.

"Of course! We're going to twirl around the rink, and maybe see a movie after. Sound good?"

Ella giggled. "Yes."

"Good night, sweetie." Ian dropped a kiss on her cheek, and then they made their way back to the kitchen where everyone was gathered.

It was a small group, but it was all the people that mattered most to both of them. Aunt Sorcha and Frank were there, along with Merry and her husband, Bill, and Cal and his wife,

Jane. The only ones who weren't able to join them were Tim and his wife, Susie, as she was due to have her baby any day and was on doctor ordered bed rest.

Ian put his arm around her and she leaned into him as they stood by the kitchen island, where there were bowls of chips and dip and a nearly empty bottle of champagne on ice. Jen looked around the room and sighed with happiness.

She'd stayed in Beauville through Christmas and flown out the day after. So, she'd been back in Dublin, at Ian's condo, for a week and it already felt like home. She missed her family, of course, but as Uncle Jim had wisely pointed out, they were "just a few plane rides away." She gave him a lesson on how to use Facebook, too, helping him put a profile up, so they could keep in touch even more easily. She'd had to laugh when all of Uncle Jim's first Facebook friends were the young waitresses that he loved to flirt with when he went out for breakfast or lunch. They all adored him.

Isabella had been excited for her and was going to handle renting out her condo. They both agreed that would be easier than trying to sell it long distance, and Isabella thought it would make a great rental and long-term investment. Mandy was thrilled for her, but disappointed, too, to lose her best friend. She was already making plans for a visit in the spring.

Her mother was initially worried about everything, the speed of their relationship and the distance, but once she met Ian and got to know him, she felt better. She was looking forward to both visiting them and having them stay with her next summer.

Merry was thrilled to have her back. "Have I mentioned how glad I am that you're going to coming into work with Ian again?" Both Jen and Merry laughed because she had mentioned it, quite a few times.

"I'm looking forward to it, too. I was really productive in that office and I missed our lunches at Max's," Jen said.

"We did fill that office with a new hire, but there happens to be an empty one right next to mine that you can probably use. Right, Ian?"

"The one the intern was using? Yeah, that should work," Ian confirmed.

Cal grinned. "Offices next to each other? That sounds like trouble! Seriously, though, glad you're back."

"Thanks, Cal."

Cal glanced at his wife and she nodded to an unspoken question.

"Ian and Jen already know this, but Jane and I have some exciting news. We're expecting our first child," Cal was beaming as he spoke and everyone offered their congratulations.

"And on that note, we're going to say good night. For the first time ever, I doubt either of us is going to see midnight tonight."

"I've been really tired these past few weeks," Jane admitted.

"We should get going, too, Frank," Aunt Sorcha said.

"Same here. We don't want to be on the roads too late," Merry said.

Ian and Jen walked everyone to the door and said their goodbyes. Aunt Sorcha pulled her in for a tight hug.

"I know I've said this already, but I am just so very happy that you came back, my dear. This is the right place for you and I know Ian feels the same."

"That I do, Mam!" Ian gave her a hug and kiss goodbye, too, and then it was just the two of them in a suddenly very quiet condo.

Jen quickly tidied up the kitchen, while Ian opened a new bottle of champagne—a special one he'd been saving for tonight. He poured them each a glass and they both stood looking out the window at the shimmering city lights below.

"This place looks great, thanks to you. Both you and my mother were right. It needed a woman's touch."

In the past week, Jen had added splashes of color here and there, to add warmth to the cool tones of the condo. She and Aunt Sorcha had gone shopping together and picked out some gorgeous watercolors for the walls and various decorative items —lamps, vases with elegant dried floral arrangements, a vintage copper wine holder for the kitchen and a few other treasures they'd discovered here and there. She'd added thick, plush soft blue towels to the bathroom and small vases of fresh flowers throughout the condo. It brightened the overall look and made it feel warm and welcoming.

"I'm glad you like it. Now it feels more like our home."

"It is our home. Yours, mine and Ella's, and I think we're going to be very happy here."

"I know we will. I don't think I've told you yet today that I love you, though. I do, you know." She smiled as she placed her free hand on his shoulder to pull him in for a kiss.

His eyes twinkled as they met hers. "I love you so much. Happy New Year, Jen. Here's to the rest of our lives together."

And then he kissed her.

THANK YOU SO MUCH FOR READING! IF YOU LIKE THIS BOOK, please check out my newest series, set on Nantucket. The Nantucket Inn is a USA Today Bestseller and my most popular book so far! I grew up on Cape Cod, near Nantucket, so this was a familiar and fun place to set a new series.

Click here to learn more!

ABOUT THE AUTHOR

Pamela M. Kelley lives in the historic seaside town of Plymouth, MA near Cape Cod. She has always been a book worm and still reads often and widely, contemporary and historical romance, suspense, and cookbooks. She writes feel good women's fiction and suspense and you'll probably see food featured and possibly a recipe or two. She is owned by a cute little shelter kitty, Bella.

Connect with Pam

pam@pamelakelley.com

Made in the USA
Monee, IL
19 January 2023

25498741R10115